THE DEVIL HIMSELF

Books by Peter Farris:
The Clay Eaters
Last Call for the Living
The Devil Himself

THE DEVIL HIMSELF

a novel

PETER FARRIS

ARCADE
CrimeWise

An Arcade CrimeWise Book

First Arcade CrimeWise Edition

Arcade Publishing books may be purchased in bulk at special discounts for sales promotion, corporate gifts, fund-raising, or educational purposes. Special editions can also be created to specifications. For details, contact the Special Sales Department, Arcade Publishing, 307 West 36th Street, 11th Floor, New York, NY 10018 or arcade@skyhorsepublishing.com.

Arcade Publishing® and CrimeWise® are registered trademarks of Skyhorse Publishing, Inc.®, a Delaware corporation.

Visit our website at www.arcadepub.com.

10 9 8 7 6 5 4 3 2 1

Library of Congress Cataloging-in-Publication Data is available on file.

ISBN: 978-1-950994-51-9

Ebook ISBN: 978-1-950994-58-8

Printed in the United States of America

Dedicated to John Linder Farris,
Pedro Jose Pasante, Ector Agnew Wright,
and Billy Wayne Donaldson
and to the memory of Marfa Strickland Donaldson
1936–2020

I'm gonna find me another home, I'm gonna find it way out in the woods. . .

—Lightnin' Hopkins, "Home in the Woods
(No Good Woman)"

At dusk the coyote crossed the hayfield, pausing every few steps to scent check the air. Prompted by a train whistle, he howled, hearing his alpha-mate and other members of the family yip and bark from the wood line to the east, followed by a collective song that rose and fell like a Dopplering siren.

The pasture had been good to him of late. He had caught and eaten a turkey poult the day before, surprising a hen leading her brood away from the nest. The poult couldn't keep up, and the hen, despite her efforts, couldn't lure the coyote away.

He slipped through a gap in the fence and made for the bottomlands. Fawns had dropped in the springtime, and he was of a mind to cruise among the water oaks and cypress trees, following the creek and staying downwind of the bedding areas along the ridges.

By nightfall, he had covered almost two miles, but the deer had moved on. The coyote caught the scent of a cottontail and followed it through thick vegetation. He came to a roadbed and turned north. Head down, nostrils flaring, he stalked toward a patch of clover and brassica.

But before he could pounce on the rabbit, his ears prickled with alarm and the coyote looked up at the firebreak. A moment later the headlights of a vehicle appeared.

The coyote stared mutely at the car before fleeing for the pinewoods, his hunt temporarily suspended.

ONE

THE GIRL IN THE TRUNK had been bound.

She slept fitfully, losing consciousness to the thrum of the interstate, only to start awake at the sound of a passing tractor trailer, jolts from ripples in the asphalt, sudden lane shifts. She could feel vibrations of the bass from a subwoofer as she sobbed.

The girl had a claustrophobic fit, grunting and kicking. The driver turned down the music, as if to listen to her struggle. She heard laughter at her expense, followed by the *boom-boom-blat* of the stereo again.

The car would slow, turn, turn again, speed up. The music stopped. She kicked at the trunk's side panels. The radio's volume swelled, loud enough to smother the racket she was raising. When the car came to a stop, the girl cocked her head, hearing voices, a brief exchange. Somebody in the car ordered a double cheeseburger. Nuggets. Fries. A chocolate shake and a diet soda.

There was a speed-bump rumble as the car jerked forward. The music kicked in again. All bass and snare and hi-hat. Synthesizers. A raspy composite of street slang and ghetto couplets.

Boom-da-boom-da-boom-boom-blat. . .

The girl in the trunk cried again, gagging on the sock in her mouth.

The car accelerated back into the metronomic flow of a freeway.

The trunk was stifling and smelled like a bedwetter's sordid pad. She had sweated through her tank top. There was a hot slick film of grit on her skin. Her head ached. The cheekbone under her left eye was tender and as raw as a rug burn. But the sweating had done her some good. She had been working her palms together, rubbing, writhing. The duct tape had loosened. She twisted her wrists, and then jerked her right arm up, pain shooting through her elbow to the shoulder, which continued to throb for a while.

But both hands were free.

Her breathing slowed as she listened, waited to see what would happen next.

But the car drove on, speakers rumbling, the sedan vibrating from bumper to bumper. An R&B hook signaled the chorus.

Boom-boom-boom-diddy-dat-dat-boom-boom-boom...

She yanked at the duct tape wrapped around her head, wrenching her jaw, pulling out hair. With her mouth uncovered she got rid of the sock and spit up bile.

After a while the girl squirmed onto her back. She lifted her legs, kneecaps knocking against the trunk roof. It was as if she was lying on a bag of rocks, tools poking her no matter what position she attempted. She groped in the darkness, fingering items like a blind person reading braille. The spare. Jumper cables. A tire iron.

And plastic sheeting. A bottle with a jug handle, like containers for bleach. A clot of industrial chain. The rough edge of a cinder block.

The bric-a-brac of a body dump.

The car maintained its steady speed.

The girl closed her eyes, thinking back to that morning. They had snatched her from the motel where all the girls lived. Her roommate—the Cambodian—screamed epithets in her native language until Lucio swung and knocked all five feet of her to the ground. Some of the others watched from the hallway but kept their mouths shut. Who could blame them? They were all cowed like dogs in a kennel.

She'd bent to help her roommate up when Lucio's partner put a hood over her head. While she was helpless, someone worked her over with a fist. That was the last she remembered—being beaten, smothering in the hood. She had probably been in the trunk of that car for hours.

She thought of one of Lucio's goons, the big one, William, who always wanted freebies. Some of the girls had talked about how sour he smelled, always blowing his nose on account of all the powder he snorted. He had a grill full of gold-lined teeth. Left the tags on his hats and clothes, a street fad at the time.

William was violent, but everybody at the motel was more scared of Lucio.

The car decelerated, exiting the interstate. Another stretch of stop and go. She sensed the driver keeping his speed down.

She figured it to be a long way from the city.

The girl wondered if normal people would think of something positive when facing their death. Like a loved one, their mother or father, a husband or boyfriend, and it might make the stark truth about their fate easier to deal with. Or maybe some special moment, a memory of good times when they were safe and life had some meaning after all.

The girl's name was Maya, and she had just turned eighteen.

She had no memories of ever being safe from the Lucios of her world.

Without the sock in her mouth, Maya reapplied the duct tape, fashioning the gag so that, she hoped, it wouldn't look as if it had been disturbed.

Her left hand slipped into a crevice beneath the spare. It closed around the handle of a six-inch screwdriver.

She cried a little, one last time.

Then she waited.

The tires skidded as the asphalt gave way to dirt, suspension flexing to bumps, mudholes, and washouts. The music stopped. She listened to the voices in the front seat.

"Should've brought a truck, four-wheel drive."

"Nah, nah, I got this."

"Give me that flashlight. I need to check the map."

"We lost?"

"Back road here leads to the ponds. Land over there belongs to the state."

"Look at all them woods. Still don't know why we don't dump the bitch right here."

Maya steeled herself against a panic attack. The car kicked into gear and continued on, crawling at times over a rough track of road. She heard tree limbs scrape against the roof and side panels of the sedan. At one point they were stalled, tires spinning in the clay of a washed-out jig. When the tires found purchase, the car lurched forward, bouncing from side to side. She was tumbled so hard her face smacked the trunk lid. But her grip on the screwdriver stayed firm. By the time the car stopped again, she had worked out a plan of attack.

Playing possum.

It had worked before with aggressive johns, the drunks and beaters, the ones who got off by smacking girls a third their size. Playing dead would give most clients pause. But the strategy didn't always produce the desired result. In a drugged-up frenzy, one guy almost threw her from a hotel balcony. Another john, assuming Maya to be unconscious or even dead, tried to put it in her behind.

An option he had not paid for.

No matter. Lucio or his muscle was always nearby—his "O-line" as he called the beefy brain-dead gangsters who protected him day and night, like a golden-armed pro quarterback. He tended to the girls as a farmer would livestock, and clients with any sense knew better than to bruise up the merchandise. Maya had heard rumors that Lucio had once castrated a man with hedge clippers to make this point.

Over time Maya learned that it had always been the normal ones who were the greatest danger, these affluent masters of the universe with their warped senses of entitlement. The lawyers or congressmen, actors and athletes who fancied their reflections in a mirror, bewitched by what they saw. Maya couldn't give a textbook definition of a sociopath, but she understood that they got ahead in life more often than most, and they had the darkest, deepest secrets to bear.

Men with appetites. Usually married. Most of them fathers.

Then there was *The Mayor*.

Maya was his favorite, at least according to Lucio. The Mayor called her *Princess. Kitten.* Let her sit on his lap and sniff powder off the nail of his pinky finger.

After their first long, sweaty night together, The Mayor asked Lucio for *exclusivity*, and from that moment on he became her sole client. When he had paid extra to brand her, Lucio didn't object. There was something peculiar about those two, Maya thought. Lucio and The Mayor shared a history, like half brothers raised in the same home, choosing different paths to reach the same goal—raw power.

Bend over. I want to see what I'm working with, The Mayor would say to her.

The night he branded her, Maya could recall his bright savage eyes as he pressed the iron into her deltoid. Took two men to hold her still. Maya almost bit through her tongue at the stink of scalded flesh. The Mayor smiled, treating the act and the moment with a solemnity his exercise of power deserved. He wiped away her tears with unexpected tenderness as the other witness to his consecration of Maya, a man with red hair and blue eyes, whispered in his ear.

We really should be going, sir.

Now Maya could feel the keloid scarring, a double *H*, the letters connected, her flesh engraved forever with the depravity of one man.

His Honor.

When the car stopped again Maya sensed it would be, for her, the last time. She breathed deeply, thinking of Lexington Market, Baltimore. Her hometown like a song she couldn't remember the words to anymore, merely the melody, something to hum. A memory of the cold dead eyes of fish lying on beds of ice provided a surge of adrenaline, the will to live.

She heard the car doors open. Maya worked her arms into their original position, preserving the illusion of bondage. She tucked the screwdriver into the small of her back and listened. A key was inserted into the lock.

Her last thought was that she had no shoes before the trunk popped open.

"Is she dead?"

Maya sensed the two men studying her.

"Nah. Baby girl ain't dead."

The man she thought must be William placed a clammy hand on her shoulder. Maya twitched. William yanked the tape from her mouth, which came off easier than he expected.

She opened her eyes to the blinding beam of a flashlight.

"All right, baby girl. Out we go."

Maya stabbed at him with the screwdriver. William jerked his hands back, smiled, and said, "What have you got there?"

Then he grabbed her wrist, torqued it until she screamed in agony, and liberated the screwdriver from her hand. He handed it to his partner, then lifted Maya from the trunk and dropped her. She hit the road hard and rolled over on her back. The stars of a clear night shone brightly above the two men.

She looked around, expecting to see Lucio, but he wasn't with them. The man with the flashlight lit a cigarette. A baleful set of eyes appeared briefly, watching her. Maya glimpsed his face, a thin mustache, and a scar slashing through one eyebrow, the names of his children tattooed in a cursive script on either side of his neck.

She looked away, working her tongue around a loosened tooth. When Maya attempted to get up, William grabbed an arm and twisted it behind her back, almost dislocating her shoulder. She tried to scream, but her throat was too dry. She made a thin, pathetic sound.

Jason looked around nervously.

"Shut her up," he said.

William laughed at his partner's show of nerves.

"Hand me that roll of tape."

Maya felt his fingers tighten around her arm. She conceived a plan, just a faint ray of hope, and turned to face him, offering up her wrists in front of her.

"Do you think we drove all the way down here so some bitch would wake up the neighborhood?" William said. "Look around you."

"Isn't this state land?"

William shook his head.

"No, this here is private property. Most of it belongs to Lucio now, like a thousand acres of timber and swampland full of gators," he said.

William gestured for the flashlight and played it around the car. Roadside scrub, tread marks, ribbons of sand and clay, what remained of a track that wouldn't take the sedan any farther. Just ahead a crude sign indicated an intersection, two planks of stave oak forming a T, the name MORNINGSTAR ROAD scored into the wood. A harvest moon illuminated the sign and late-summer growth beyond.

Jason looked again at Maya lying in parched stiff grass beside the road, breathing hard and staring back at him. He bit his lip uneasily.

"She is one fine piece," he said.

William grinned. "No doubt,"

"What did she do to deserve this?" Jason said.

"Don't matter. Lucio says she's gone—then she's gone."

William passed the flashlight's beam across the closely packed pines to his right. A flurry of moths flickered in the light.

Jason nudged Maya, who flinched but didn't take her eyes off him.

"Man," he lamented, adjusting himself. "What I'd give to feel a piece like this raw. Grade-A senator's pussy right here."

"You want a taste before we get to work, fine by me," William said, no stranger himself to free samples while a girl was in transit or waiting to be sold.

"Yeah?"

"Long as you get it done while I piss."

He walked toward a patch of broom sedge before adding, "But don't be puttin' it in her mouth 'less you feel like losin' it."

Jason picked her up by the arms, pushed her head sideways against the trunk lid. He was sucking night air through his teeth. Maya retreated to the place in her mind where she went when men were on top of her, between her, behind her. Groping, nibbling, biting, burning her, half-strangling her, whispering words that they would never whisper to any other woman.

For Maya it was like dropping a coffin lid on herself before the first shovelful of dirt.

One last time, she thought.

Jason pulled his dick from his pants, and then spit into his hand.

A sound came from the woods, the sonorous hoot of a barred owl. A deer barked and crashed off into the brush. Jason turned his head, temporarily distracted. Maya seized his distraction, whirled in one motion, then kicked him hard in the groin. Jason fell sideways, clutched his balls, and groaned.

And Maya was gone, bare feet kicking up dust, her body backlit by the sedan's headlights.

"Oh, shit," William said.

He had been smoking a cigarette, planning to watch Jason have his way with the girl, when she made her move. She had a good head start, too. William ditched the cigarette and flashed his light on Maya.

But William, a hundred pounds overweight, couldn't truck in baggy sweats. He barely kept Maya in range of his light as she abandoned the road, cutting behind a clump of dog fennel and into the darkness of a pine thicket. William followed, blind but not deaf to her whereabouts. He lumbered through brush and thorny weeds, feeling the briars grab at his sweatpants.

After a hundred yards he stopped among some hardwoods, winded, shining the light around and listening. He played the light off the canopy of oaks above the forest understory. For a few seconds William thought he might have lost her for good. He knew she was barefoot, and the bottomlands were thick with windfalls and cottonmouths. No easy place for her to hide.

Then he heard her shriek and took off at two o'clock.

Maya tripped on a rotted log and fell. On hands and knees she clamored forward into some greenbrier vines. The thorny spines clung to her, piercing her arms and neck. She cried out, her pant legs ensnared by the vines. With a frantic kick she freed herself and emerged on the other side of the thicket.

At the sound of footfalls, she looked back and saw William's lumbering form, the flashlight wanding through the dark. Maya climbed down into a gulley and slid behind a sweet gum. Gasped when her foot came down on the spiky balls of fruit littering the base of the tree. She peered around the trunk, looking up at the ridgeline, disoriented, no bearing or knowledge of where she was or how to get out of these woods. She tried to catch her breath, and then began chewing at the tape around her wrists.

"It's okay, baby girl. I'm not going to hurt you no more," William said, hoofing it along the ridge. He clucked his tongue a few times. After a few minutes he looked down into a draw where he saw a meandering creek.

"I got a message from Lucio," he said. "Called the whole thing off. It's all a *big* mistake. We're going back home now. Just come to me, and we can forget all this shit. You hear me, Maya? I know you're out there listening."

William stopped. Heard running water and passed the flashlight across a few birch trees down near the banks of the creek. Fifty yards away, he thought he glimpsed a shoulder peeking out from behind a tree trunk and allowed the light to linger.

Maya glimpsed him then, a shadow in the moonwash creeping closer. In her panic she was too eager to believe him.

"You mean that?" she said.

William stopped and stared in her direction, like a cat hearing a random noise and of a mind to investigate.

"Yeah, baby girl. Look here."

He pulled out a flip phone. The display screen glowed an icy blue in the darkness. He waved it slowly back and forth a couple of times. With her cheek pressed against the scaly furrows of the sweet gum's bark, Maya took a quick look and then ducked behind the tree again.

"We use a code," he said. "Numbers here mean Lucio is callin' it all off. Everything's going to be all right."

Maya bit her lip, biting back a surge of tears.

When she could talk without her voice breaking she said, "What about Jason?"

William didn't answer. She heard him take a few steps, the crunch of leaves underfoot. He was still about fifty yards away and Maya saw his flashlight sweeping across the trees on either side of the creek. Slow, steady progress cut the distance to her by a third before he answered.

"Don't worry about Jason," he finally said.

He let that sink in for a few seconds. "Lucio will make things right. No need to worry, baby girl."

She sensed that he was edging closer. Off in the distance a coyote yipped and a nearby den erupted in song. Startled, William let out a little gasp.

His talk of codes reminded Maya of the fact that Lucio didn't like phones. Never trusted them for business, and business had brought her to this moment. She knew if William could get a hand on her he would kill her right where she stood.

Maya got up and ran deeper into the murky creek bottom, the mud sucking at her feet. She heard William in pursuit and turned east, climbing upslope through leafy marl until she hit a barbwire fence along the ridge top. She followed it for a time. Glimpsed a small woodlot ahead, a clear-cut beyond it, what looked like a field thick with goldenrod glimmering in the moonlight. At a low spot in the wire Maya hopped the fence but tripped. A barb opened a gash on her ankle. She choked on a scream and continued haltingly toward the field.

She turned and saw the flashlight near the fence, William hustling along trying to find a spot to climb over. That's when he stopped, pointed a Beretta nine-millimeter at her, and started shooting.

Maya took cover behind a red oak, and a moment later a bullet missed her head by inches. Her body felt heavy and uncoordinated.

She heard two voices coming from the creek bottom now. Looking back, she saw William in pursuit, wriggling under the barbwire, a shiny nickel-plated pistol in his hand. Jason appeared behind him with an obvious limp, cursing her. Maya left the cover of the oak and ran toward a logging road that skirted the clear-cut. On the other side was a field. A few hundred yards beyond that, she saw some sort of homestead—she wasn't sure if she was seeing the roof of a house or of a barn.

Maya ran blindly into the pasture and then shrieked at the sight of a seven-foot scarecrow, one of several she quickly realized, the stuffed bodies hanging from X-shaped crosses and draped with twisted vine. The scarecrow's head was cocked to one side, as if it were asleep on a train, mouth fashioned into a crinkled grin. Its round unblinking eyes seemed starkly real.

"Listen. Hear that?"

She looked back and saw William's flashlight. He took another shot at her as she dodged away from the malign scarecrow.

"Hold still, baby girl!" William called across the field.

Maya had obeyed similar orders from every man who paid for her, their right of possession. She hesitated for a moment, the scarecrows a new kind of fright to deal with, unaware that Jason had diverged from William and was circling to her right, bent over in tall grass, even more eager than William to kill her. When she heard a gunshot from another direction, Maya vaulted over the scarecrow and made for the house at the end of the field, where kerosene lamps burned in two windows. Flickers of light where there hadn't been light seconds ago.

At least a dozen crucified scarecrows haunted the pasture, threadbare robes swaying in a breeze. What they were all about Maya didn't know, but dodging through and around the scarecrows made it more difficult for either William or Jason to draw a bead on her.

Gasping, she emerged from the field and followed a dirt path to a barn. There was a low windmill beside it, the house not much farther away. Maya ran toward the house, her heart thumping like a flat tire. She was thirty yards from the front door when Jason lumbered out from behind a shed, blindside, and drove Maya to the ground.

"How you like that?"

As she squirmed under him, he punched her in the gut. Maya pulled her knees up, deflecting more blows while Jason raged at her.

Jason suddenly shoved a revolver in her face, chipping a tooth. Maya grimaced, looking at Jason's face as he cocked the pistol. She had no more fight in her. Her breathing slowed. She felt a welcome sense of calm.

"Do it," she said. "Get it over, then."

"I aim to," Jason said.

She heard another man's voice answer him.

"Don't think so, son. I do all the wrecking in this here joint."

Maya saw the pistol fly off as Jason's head was turned violently around by a blow from a rifle stock. She heard the snap of a jawbone and blood sprayed into her eyes as Jason fell off her.

TWO

SHE DIDN'T KNOW IT WAS called lucid dreaming, but that's what Maya was doing. She was a bird dog tracking a succession of scents, nose to the ground, the odors not gamey but pleasant, and all from her childhood, a bag of movie theater popcorn, gummy candy, Mary Sue chocolates. She lingered in places, burrowing her snout into earth as soft as baking flour. But something called to her in the dream, whistling, like a melody from her subconscious, reminding her of a task to complete. There was a sack that hung from her neck requiring delivery.

But what was it? And who was it for?

She came to a trail and followed it into an alluvial forest. Could feel the soft thud as her paws struck the duff. Her tongue hung loose in a heavy, healthy pant. There was a stream ahead and she stopped at the bank to drink. *I am home*, she thought, controlling the twitch of her tail by simply thinking about it.

I am home.

Maya woke up.

She was in a bedroom, sunlight filtering through nicotine-stained curtains. The linens were clean, but musty with age, as if they had been unearthed from storage and put on the bed without first being aired. She touched a hand to her sore dry lips and winced. A bandage covered her left eye. She felt a large spot on the pillowcase where she had drooled in her sleep. She worked her sore jaw and then pulled the sheet down and stretched.

Her feet hurt like hell, too. Maya looked down at them and was surprised to find the wound on her ankle had been cleaned and dressed. Her eyes glazed over, remembering her escape, the faces of William and Jason, and the question as to who had all but knocked Jason's brains out of his head with a gunstock.

Where was Jason now, she thought, looking around? And William? More important, *where was she?*

There was a solid pine nightstand next to the bed, its surfaces chipped, the legs poorly repaired, as if the stand had been relocated through the years by being thrown out of windows. On the table someone had left a jelly jar of water, some aspirin, tissue, and cotton cloths that smelled of rubbing alcohol and were stained with dried blood. Maya grimaced, feeling a burning in her abdomen, an ache in her lower back. She pressed down on her gut until the cramp passed. She reached for the jar and took a sip, then tapped two aspirin from the bottle into her palm.

Now, outside the bedroom windows, purple martins were in full song. Maya looked out at the yard and saw the birds flying around a hanging city of gourds. Elsewhere, chickens scratched and pecked at the ground. After a few moments she got out of bed and limped to the door. Cocked her head and heard the clatter of pots and pans. Smelled bacon frying.

Maya looked around the room again and walked over to an antique dresser. Took a long look at herself in the mirror. Then she opened a drawer to find more than a dozen men's wallets arranged neatly in two rows. She picked one up, opened it and pulled out a long-expired driver's license. So old there was no photograph of the operator.

Maya discovered IDs in each, the licenses issued in a different name for almost every state east of the Mississippi, the brown leather dry and creased like the knuckles of old people. Whether they had been stolen or forged, she didn't know.

She closed the drawer. Her attention was drawn to a crack in the door and the cat that had slunk into the bedroom. It regarded her coolly before hopping onto the windowsill.

Maya left the room and walked the length of a short hallway, putting as little weight on her sore right heel as possible. A kitten appeared and ran down the staircase, disappeared around the corner. Maya gripped the handrail, the polished wood creaking loudly. She wondered if someone in the kitchen had heard.

There was a small foyer at the bottom of the stairs. A pump-action shotgun was propped beside the front door.

Yet another cat showed itself, this one an adult, its slender black body reminding Maya of a painting The Mayor had in his private study. "An original Steinlen," he had boasted. The cat in the painting had unruly whiskers and big yellow eyes, an inscription in French but The Mayor never offered to explain its meaning as she was being taken to a waiting car, still smarting from their session that evening.

In the kitchen the man had his back to Maya. Something sizzled in a cast-iron skillet. The air was rich with the aroma of breakfast meats. Maya took a couple steps toward a table, and then stopped at the sight of a mannequin dressed in Sunday best, seated before a spread of baskets, platters, and cutlery as if she had every intention of dining. There was an unlit cigarette in an ashtray.

The man looked around at Maya, although she hadn't made a sound. His mouth pulled to one side in a smile.

"Morning," he said.

Maya nodded. The man had a lanky body. His face was narrow, clean-shaven, with a beaked nose perfectly suited for the wire-frame spectacles he wore. Looked to Maya as if he cut his thinning gray hair himself. He was older from her perspective and experience with men, but looked physically fit, with the aura only intelligent men generated. Occasionally she'd had one like him, but for the most part her clients had been vulnerable and pathetic in their needs.

Maya glanced from the man to the mannequin at the kitchen table, and then back to the pistol he wore on his hip in a leather holster with a buttoned flap.

He said, "When you got no friends like me, it's advisable to carry a gun."

Maya's eyes fell to her bare feet. They were filthy enough to have tracked dirt on his floor. She began to cry.

"I'm sorry," she said.

"Sorry for being hungry, I hope. Sit you down."

When Maya hesitated, he gestured curtly at the table, then pointed to a chair to the right of the mannequin.

"My name's Leonard."

She took her seat. He brought plates of food to the table.

"Hope you like hoecakes, cracklin' bread, bacon, sausage, and eggs," Leonard said. "Peppermint sticks for after should you fancy. Marjean loves her peppermint, don't you, darling?"

Maya looked over at the mannequin, thinking if she were dead and this Hell, you couldn't fault the devil for having a sense of humor.

"Go on now," Leonard insisted. "I'm not the best cook, but I ain't going to poison you, either."

Leonard poured coffee from an old tin pot, then stopped to kiss the mannequin's cheek. He filled Maya's glass with orange juice, then got up and retrieved from the refrigerator a pitcher of milk, cream thick as a finger floating on the surface. Leonard sat down again. Looked around as if he had forgotten something. Maya didn't move, her expression of weary acceptance not unlike that of an animal unexpectedly rescued and sheltered.

He tilted his head back as if to see her better through his spectacles.

"So, young lady, what do I call *you*?"

"My name's Maya," she said softly.

"That's a pretty name."

He looked at the mannequin and smiled as if it had spoke. He turned to Maya.

"Are you hungry, Maya?"

She nodded, but the worry in her face was raw as a wound.

"Are you thinking about them men from last night?"

Lips trembling, Maya nodded. Under the table, a cat rubbed up leisurely against her shin.

"Do you see those men around here now?"

Maya wiped her eyes and shook her head. Leonard smiled, an air of satisfaction coming into his face.

"I'm always ravenous," he said, "after I deliver an Old Testament ass-whooping."

He loaded up her plate with hoecakes and syrup, sausage links, grits soaked in a bath of runny egg yolk. He put the plate in front of Maya, and then took one of the mannequin's hands in his and closed his eyes. After the brief prayer, he lit the cigarette in the ashtray and let it smolder while they ate.

"Marjean likes to smoke with every meal," he said by way of explanation.

Maya looked from Leonard to the mannequin. *Marjean* wore a long blue gingham farm dress. There was an ill-fitting wig on her head. Someone had applied makeup in a crude attempt to conceal a divot in the nose, faded paint on her cheeks, a few scratches and cosmetic imperfections on the chin and neck. But the plaster head was far from lifelike. The mannequin seemed to stare at Maya with an expression indifferent as a dirt dauber's.

Her appetite overwhelmed whatever worries Maya felt. It had been two days since she had last eaten. She drained the glass of milk, and then gulped juice and coffee between forkfuls of food. She took the sausage apart with her fingers and dipped pieces of it in the grits and syrup. Leonard watched her eat with a bemused expression.

"Somebody have you on a strict diet?"

Thinking of Lucio cost her what was left of her appetite. But her plate was nearly empty. Maya nodded without looking up.

"My—my *boyfriend* used to weigh me," she said.

Leonard arched an eyebrow.

"That so?"

"Yeah."

He offered Maya a cigarette from the pack by the ashtray. Wasn't a menthol like she preferred, but she accepted it gratefully. Her hands trembled, so Leonard took the box of matches from her, lit her cigarette before lighting his own.

"I would have called the law but I don't believe in 'em," he said. "Or trust 'em."

Maya looked at him. She blinked away smoke from her own cigarette.

"You scare those men away?"

Leonard crossed his arms and leaned back in his chair, glancing at Marjean as if she were about to interrupt.

"Something like that."

"They wanted to kill me."

"Why?"

Maya didn't answer. Leonard studied her with a hint of sympathy.

"How old are you?"

"I turned eighteen last week."

"Lord have mercy," Leonard said, as if he wasn't quite sure he believed her.

Maya hunched her shoulders, not looking at him.

"You got any family? Someone you can call? I don't keep a telephone out here, but there's quite a few in town."

"No family," Maya said, keeping her head down, noting the unmistakable scorn in his voice. She was trembling again.

"Why did those men want to kill you, Maya?"

She bit her lip. *What had he said about trust and the police?*

Maya glanced at the mannequin again and then closed her eyes, thinking how she had seen abnormal in all of its manifestations. Kinky, depraved behavior, perverted passions, men on all fours in full rut, their privates long and wrinkled at the end like an anteater's snout or stubby as mushrooms. By fifteen Maya was certain nothing in life could shock her again.

But the unease she felt after a half hour with Leonard was a warning.

After a few minutes, she got up from the table with a nod of thanks. Leonard watched her, smoking his cigarette. She lingered by the kitchen door for a moment. Looked at her feet again.

"Don't suppose you got any shoes?"

"Reckon none that will fit. Marjean got whoppers, don't you, dear?"

"Okay. I should be going."

"Where are you going?"

"Got to keep moving. That's all."

"Okay then. Take the road a ways out. It's a quite a trek. Just follow the tire tracks and watch them brush piles. Killed a copperhead the other day and the babies are out this time of year. When you get to the first firebreak you make a right."

Maya nodded and reached for the doorknob. She offered one last look at Leonard and the mannequin.

"Thanks for the breakfast," she said. "Never ate so much."

Leonard didn't answer, just sat there smoking, eyes narrowed.

She left the house through the kitchen door and walked into the yard. She found a rubber band in the pocket of her jeans and used it to bind her hair off her neck. Without looking back she made her way beneath the hanging gourds she had seen from the bedroom window, nesting materials littering the ground, the grass prickly against her skin. The chickens scurried away from her, and near the edge of the field a family of does regarded Maya for a moment and then disappeared into the brush. She followed a one-track road of red clay away from the house. Her feet were covered in scratches and blisters.

The going was slow, Maya bewildered by her predicament, the choices ahead, all of them bad. She yearned for some codeine cough syrup, or vodka, anything to dull the panic building inside her. It was warm, and ghost-swarms of gnats were drawn to her cuts and scabs, to her mouth and eyes. She looked west across the field where carrion birds circled high. She could see a few scarecrows languishing in the summer sun, heads canted to one side, sugar-sack faces leaking straw. Yellow jackets cruised near her. There was thick timber in every direction. She looked back at the homestead and thought she saw Leonard in the yard now, a column of smoke rising from a burn barrel.

The clay drive forked, and, not sure of her direction, she headed west toward the field. The road was rutted and been reshaped for the worse by heavy rain. In the sky, more birds circled. She spotted a clear-cut with a large slash pile that seemed familiar. Had she run past it the previous night? Buzzards lined the limbs of an ash tree, watching the pile with interest.

Something glimmered on the ground among the brush and sun-bleached limbs, reflecting the light like a sunbather.

Maya left the road to take a closer look. Thought she saw a flee-ing rodent, then an arm and a leg among the branches, a body naked and rigidly preserved like a piece of performance art, and then she thought that Jason was looking at her, his skin alive with undulating clusters of fire ants.

Her scream startled an armadillo from the anthill beneath Jason's naked corpse.

Maya ran.

Leonard was stoking the fire in the burn barrel with a three-tined hayfork when she appeared in the distance. He watched her limp toward back the house, favoring her right leg, her face wild with fright. She disappeared behind the barn where he kept parts for his still, then reappeared at a much slower pace as she approached the yard, passing the well he had dug with a pick and shovel forty feet deep and curbed with cypress boards.

Wind chimes on the porch played a little tune, as if Maya had brought a breeze with her. Leonard smiled.

"Reckon you might want to stay for lunch?"

Maya's eyes darted to the pair of sneakers piled at Leonard's feet along with the sweatpants that had belonged to William. Leonard stuck a sneaker with the pitchfork and fed it to the barrel.

"You did that?" she said, looking back in the direction of Jason's final resting place.

Leonard shrugged.

"Fat one got away before I could humiliate him further. He won't say nothing, to the law anyhow. I do have that effect on people."

"But you killed him? Killed Jason."

Leonard stabbed the other sneaker, and then twirled the soiled sweatpants around the fork tines. He dumped the last of William's clothes in the fire. Jabbed the pitchfork into the ground.

"So that was his name? Figured it was Horse's Ass."

"Huh?"

Leonard smiled, without humor.

"I know one when I see one."

Tense with shock, Maya stood there shaking. She took a step back and winced.

"I don't understand."

"I don't know what this man *did*," Leonard said, pointing to the world beyond his tract as if it were as alien to him as another solar system. "But nobody comes around here without my permission. And you sure as hell don't harm a woman on my property. Understand? It's *my* law here. *My* justice."

Maya raised her head, looking around the homestead again, then, reluctantly at Leonard, weighing the hospitality of a psychopath against the cruel life she had temporarily escaped. Hunted by a pimp and burdened with the secret of his most powerful patron.

She finally met Leonard's eyes. Pale, unblinking, but not unkind. She could smell the noxious burn of William's clothes in the barrel. *What did Leonard want with her? He had to want something.*

They all did.

Still holding his patient gaze, giving nothing by way of an expression, Maya said, "So what's for lunch?"

THREE

Deputy Jack Chalmers was chewing on a handful of pecans when the Caprice passed him at twenty over the limit. Chalmers was parked between a church and its cemetery, on a gravel drive obscured by pine trees, a speed trap that was one of Trickum County's major sources of revenue.

He hit the lights and wheeled his patrol car onto the highway. The only other traffic was a tractor trailer from the brewery, on its way to Tallahassee or Tuscaloosa. He saw the black Caprice again and speeded up close, getting a glance from the man behind the wheel in the rearview before the driver signaled, pulled onto a wide breakdown lane, and cut the engine.

The plates on the Caprice were legitimate. Car was registered to a Lucille Watkins in Fulton County. Long way from home, Chalmers thought. He stepped out of his cruiser. Adjusted his campaign hat, aware of the man's eyes watching him in the side-view mirror, hands at noon on the wheel. Approaching from the driver's seven o'clock, Chalmers could tell the man wasn't wearing a shirt. With his hand on his service weapon, Chalmers closed the distance to the car, blading himself near the back door.

The man inside the Caprice was huge, three hundred pounds, and appeared to be not just shirtless, but bare-ass naked.

And bleeding.

His face, chest, and arms were crisscrossed with scratches. A hamburger wrapper covered his crotch.

"Hidy," Chalmers said, watching the driver closely. "Got a driver's license on you?"

The man obliged, slowly reaching for a wallet on the dashboard. He offered the car registration and license with a deliberate turn of his left hand.

"Know why I pulled you over?"

The driver's eyes were vacant. He pursed his lips and nodded.

Chalmers studied the license, and then spoke into the radio clipped above his collarbone, leading with the number and issue date.

"Dispatch. Check for possible 10-27, 10-99."

He glanced in the back seat, then to the driver, Chalmers's attention to William Watkins so focused a satellite could've probably picked up its intensity. Guy had to be on something. PCP or hallucinogens was Chalmers's first guess. The car? Stolen, his gut told him. William was stoic. Not entirely present, in the way Chalmers's wife would accuse him of being sometimes. Mind still on the job or the lake or troubled by some memory not worth reliving.

"You all right, Mr. Watkins?"

William nodded and looked straight ahead.

Reminded Chalmers of a diabetic whiteout call he had responded to once. Middle-aged male who had been in the sun all day playing golf. Suffering from low blood sugar, he became belligerent, aggressive, and received a face full of pepper spray for resisting arrest. By the time paramedics gave him the go-juice the diabetic could remember nothing of his episode and asked why his hands were cuffed. Chalmers guessed this William in front of him was still coming to grips with a recent trauma.

"Signal Five, are you 10-12?" dispatch said, asking Chalmers if he was clear for radio traffic. Chalmers was reasonably sure that Mr. Watkins—if that's who he was—didn't know police ten codes. He looked borderline catatonic, not even interested in batting away the gnats gathered on his bloody arms.

"Go ahead, Dispatch."

"Valid, no wants."

"Copy," Chalmers said. He looked down at William and smiled again. "Mind telling me why you don't have any clothes on, Mr. Watkins?"

William shook his head, a gesture that Chalmers read not so much as an answer to his question but as an expression of disbelief. It wasn't even ten in the morning, and the deputy had a naked man the size of a forklift on his hands. William Watkins technically had not done anything wrong, either. Driving nude, unless that nudity was displayed to the public, wasn't a violation. Chalmers couldn't smell alcohol, or any other controlled substance for that matter. Just ripe man-flesh. The deputy could request the county's drug recognition expert to help him with a field investigation, but that could take all day. Reminded Chalmers of something the sheriff used to tell him.

You can beat the rap but you can't beat the ride.

Chalmers knew he was going to have to get creative.

"What happened to you?"

William shook his head and stared out the window.

I won't tell you, he seemed to say. *Wouldn't believe me if I did.*

Chalmers had an obligation, however, to continue this investigation until his suspicions were dispelled. Finding a way to keep the naked man from just driving away.

And on cue, William said, "Am I free to go, or am I being detained?"

"No. You're not free to go. Would you like me to call an ambulance for you?"

No answer.

"Look at me," Chalmers said, more forceful now.

William cocked an eye in Chalmers's direction.

"Come on. Fight with your old lady, right? Or got run off by somebody's husband? Maybe picked up a gal at the bar last night? Getting busy and she pulls a piece, robs you blind? Wouldn't be the first time it's happened."

Chalmers looked up as another cruiser pulled over.

William saw the second patrol car in the rearview mirror and sighed. Gnats swarmed him, drawn to the dried blood and abrasions along his arms and chest. A tractor trailer whizzed by, the trucker sitting high inside the cab, offering a wave to ol' Smokey and his customer. It gave Chalmers an idea.

"Step out of the vehicle."

He opened the driver's-side door. William hesitated and then shrugged and eased out of the sedan, putting his hands behind his back without having to be asked.

Right about the time a church van came over the hill.

The driver from Mount Bethel Baptist Church slowed, and Chalmers estimated about a dozen elderly women were inside the van but there could have been more, the ladies within getting an eyeful as William slumped into the back of the cruiser.

Mickey Summerlin, Chalmers's backup, gave William a nudge to slide over and closed the door. He looked at his hand, and then wiped it on a pant leg.

"Prayer group should be lively tonight."

"Oh, Christ."

"That is one big, bad bio risk you got there, Jack."

Chalmers sucked on a tooth. A green beer bottle twinkled in the roadside scrub. He couldn't disagree.

"Every day is a full moon on my shift."

"Welcome to Trickum, bud. What's the charge?"

"Public nudity."

Summerlin smiled. Already sweat stains arced out from the armpits of his forest-green uniform blouse.

"You ready?" Chalmers said, nodding to the Caprice.

"Uh-huh. We going to book them as accessories?" Summerlin said, pointing to the flies crawling on the windows inside his patrol car.

Chalmers and Summerlin did a full search of the sedan and had begun an inventory when the tow truck arrived.

The car was clean for weapons and drugs. No explosives. It was safe for storage.

But the contents of the Caprice's trunk were giving Chalmers a bad case of "something doesn't look right."

"Now what's a guy like William doing all the way down here with 30-proof coil steel chain, plastic sheeting, and two cinder blocks?" he said.

Summerlin whistled. He was initialing the inventory sheet, which eventually would go into William's property bag along with his license, registration card, a pack of cigarillos, and a set of keys attached to the Falcon mascot of Atlanta's pro football franchise.

"Reeks of bleach, doesn't it?" he said, not looking up from the clipboard.

"He'll probably just say he left the bottle open and it spilled."

"If he has any brains, he would," Summerlin said. "You smell something besides the bleach?"

"Yeah."

Chalmers looked closer inside the trunk, seeing nothing. The bleach was making his nose run.

"Don't think the bleach spilled. The whole trunk has been scrubbed down."

"Not against the law to clean your trunk."

Chalmers shook his head. Summerlin removed his reading glasses and looked back down the road.

"You think a bleached trunk and drop cloth means there's a body out there somewhere, don't you?"

"I do."

"And how would *that* be any of our concern?" Summerlin deadpanned.

Chalmers glanced at William, partially obscured by the patrol car's wire partition. William sat upright, his eyes closed, as if he were dozing at a funeral. Gnats crawled everywhere.

"I'm going to put a hold on the vehicle," Chalmers said, and, noting Summerlin's hangdog expression, clarified his interest.

"Suspicious circumstances."

"You can run that one by Prance," Summerlin said indifferently. "I've got us a dirt road to po-lice."

William Watkins was booked and processed at the Trickum County jail, a giant concrete building that had all the charm of a staph infection. He received a paper jumpsuit and slippers known as "Nikes" by Trickum's witty repeat offenders, and was placed in a holding cell for drunks and nonviolent misdemeanor suspects.

Meanwhile Chalmers radioed the captain of the investigative division, Ronnie Prance.

"Car's clean?" Prance said.

Chalmers heard billiard balls being racked in the background.

"Yes, sir."

"No blood? No sign of trauma?"

"All there in my report."

"Well, I'm not in my office. But the car's clean you said?"

Chalmers pulled the phone away from his ear when the detective coughed.

"It is."

"Write it up. Send it up," Prance said.

Four hours later William Watkins posted bond, collected his belongings, and drove away, still wearing the orange paper jumpsuit.

The head jailer told Chalmers that the man hadn't spoken during his jail time, except for a brief call to an attorney in Atlanta.

William had gotten away with one, and Chalmers knew it.

He jotted down the name of the lawyer, checked his watch, and poured himself a cup of coffee, wondering what weirdness out there in the county was about to find him next.

FOUR

His name was Lucio Cottles.

As a youth he roamed abandoned lots and squatter homes south of English Avenue, eating out of dumpsters, dousing cats in brake fluid and lighting them on fire, shaking down kids twice his age. When some resisted, he attacked them with a rusty machete.

He laughed derisively the first time someone took a shot at him.

Nobody knew what to do with Lucio. At a hearing with the Department of Juvenile Justice, one administrator privately remarked that the best place for him might be at the bottom of the Chattahoochee River.

If they had overheard the remark, most arresting officers would have agreed.

Without much effort, Lucio made it to Hays State Prison, where he learned from the best and eventually took over Y Dorm. Once out of Hays, he returned to English Avenue and ganged up quickly. With a knack for survival, he recruited the desperate and unsupervised. Youthful zombies and streetwalkers, Lucio's hood a world of few leaders and ample followers.

He and his crew started small, smash and grabs for designer jeans. Next came the carjackings and home invasions.

Then, like a college grad surveying the job market, Lucio found his true niche in life.

Prostitution.

He had a talent for reading kids, especially young girls. They were drawn to him, too, his good looks and outré thuggishness, a glare that could ignite the phosphorous head of a match. Lucio knew their weaknesses and took special pleasure in breaking down his victims. He was cruel but sympathetic by turn. Because of that paradoxical but effective combination of violence and tenderness the girls were loyal to him.

They called him *Daddy.*

The money was good, but Lucio had become addicted to that look in a woman's eyes when she had lost all hope.

His earnings were funneled into legitimate service-based businesses. Spas. Barbershops. Motels. Escort services.

A juicehead pastor from a megachurch was his first celebrity client.

Two teenage girls for twelve hours.

Soon every player on the Southside came to him for pussy. Lucio recruited most of the girls personally, a few he kidnapped. He kept them drugged and moved them around like cattle. They came from all over—Oakland, Chicago, the DC–Philly–New York–Boston corridor, even Cancún and Tampico. White. Black. Latina. Filipino. Russian. Romanian. Runaways. Illegals. He eventually took his product on the road. In the early days of the internet he had geek-hacker-pedophiles on his payroll, helping him to establish a nationwide network, catering to the sexually ravenous.

Pervs in upper tax brackets.

Then he franchised. New Orleans. Memphis. Las Vegas.

In his hometown he donated heavily to the Fraternal Order of Police.

Rumor was he had The Mayor's ear.

From one of the Russian girls Lucio learned the word *kompromat* and began to keep dirt on all his clients. Used the blackmail to his advantage. Audio, video, files upon files of career-killing, marriage-ending, reputation-shredding, life-threatening dirt. Knowing America never applied justice equally, he hired the best lawyers money could buy.

Cowboys from state and federal came after him. They got nowhere.

Unlike his peers, Lucio had little use for material things. He loathed fancy cars and jewelry. Spurned the street threads with gaudy designs that were all the rage. Not his style.

Instead Lucio lived like a monk, a slave to discipline. He read voraciously and kept to a strict vegetarian diet. Abstained from alcohol and drugs while pumping his girls with both. He floated between austere apartments and safe houses, his schedule as unpredictable as an earthquake. In addition to street muscle a small cadre of ex–law enforcement honchos attended to his personal security and well-being.

Lucio had once read that corporations had more rights than individuals. He disappeared into the monolithic shadows cast by shell companies. He legitimized, investing in soundstages near Hapeville and a recording studio on 11th Street, and after meeting the man with the snakeskin boots, Lucio began to buy prime acreage down south.

One alligator-infested tract served as the final resting place for those who had displeased or disrespected him.

Nothing, Lucio often mused, goes to waste in the wild.

When William Watkins walked through the door of Limelight Tattoo, Lucio had been thinking about all those bloated bodies. His guest, the man from Tamaulipas with the snakeskin boots, was watching the tattoo artist work round shader needles into Lucio's flesh.

The artist wiped blood and ink from above Lucio's wrist and leaned back, eyeballing the outline of a dead bird with worms dangling from its beak, tapping the foot switch in rhythm with music on the stereo. Miles Davis in a righteous jazz-rock freakout.

It was a Sunday, and Lucio and Snakeskin had the place to themselves. After all, Lucio owned it.

A pair of bodyguards and Lucio's head of security, Gregory Grimes, met William at the door. William whispered to Grimes and then stood back and waited. Bit his bottom lip and tried to keep his hands from shaking. The parlor smelled of tincture of green soap and latex. He looked around blankly at the walls of flash art.

"He's got company, you know?" Grimes said.

"It's important," William said.

"Wait here."

Grimes disappeared around the partition, said a few words, and then reappeared and waved William over to the booth.

They walked behind a partition and William saw the man with the snakeskin boots, noted the general air of danger about him. The man stared at William but said nothing.

William dropped his eyes. Neither Lucio nor Snakeskin acknowledged him as the artist continued to work the tattoo gun near Lucio's wrist, fanning the needles back and forth below the dermis. A painful spot, as William recalled from his last time in the chair, having had the Louis Vuitton pattern inked from the meat of his shoulder to the top of his right hand. But that pain hadn't compared to the alcohol bath advised by Lucio's in-house physician. William cleared his throat.

"I'm proud of you," Lucio finally said.

William's face tightened. Figured it was going to go one of two ways for him.

"What are you proud of me for?"

Lucio looked up at him and smiled.

"What are you thinking about?"

William shrugged. "A .22 with an orange juice bottle silencer just behind my right ear."

"That's good," Lucio said. "Given the predicament in which you found yourself, you could have panicked. But you kept your nerve. And your mouth shut."

"What happened down there?" Snakeskin said.

"Who's asking?" William said.

"Answer the question," Lucio said.

The tattoo artist cocked his head, went *buzz buzz buzz* with the foot switch as if contributing to the conversation, and etched a path of black ink near Lucio's elbow joint.

"I don't know what to say."

"Try."

"She got away. And then some old swamper got the jump on Jason and me. Tied me to the back of his truck and drug me across a field. Damn near killed me, but the rope broke, and I managed to get away."

"Where's Jason now?"

"Dead—I think."

"And Maya?"

"Hiding out in this house way out near the swamp."

"A neighbor of mine?" Lucio said.

"Of ours," Snakeskin said and smiled. "You know, Lucio, where I am from country people are not to be trifled with."

William nodded. "I'll make this right," he said. "Give me another chance. I'll stuff that bitch in an alligator's mouth myself."

The drone of the tattoo gun broke off for a beat. Lucio met William's eyes and grinned, the look of a man stoned on endorphins and enjoying the mood of easy menace that accompanied him every-where. William wiped his leaking nose with a palm and bore the weight of the silence that followed, feeling the drone of the tattoo gun in his heart.

"Got a fix where it all went wrong?" Lucio said.

"Yeah. I do."

"Grimes will go with you."

"I'll make the plate and serve her up."

"You'll actually make *two*," Lucio said.

"Two?"

"Maya's guardian angel, of course."

His chief of staff held the door open as The Mayor and a coterie exited the conference room, an entourage multiplying from one end of the hall to the other. The chief operating officer, communica-tions liaison, and various aides joined their group. A red-haired man named Eric Lambert was close by as well, walking in step with The Mayor, face-scanning, his expression that of someone assuming the worst about the near future.

A three-car convoy waited outside.

The Mayor had just delivered a closed-door, bare-knuckle ulti-matum to the city school board. Accreditation issues. Infighting. A testing scandal. It was one of a hundred political headaches that never resolve themselves, issues that occasionally went into remission or mutated but would return with the frequency of spring rainfall.

Next on his agenda: the State of the City breakfast.

The Mayor looked out the window of the sport utility, absently turning the college class ring on his finger. He had remained in New Haven for law school, waded into the private sector, and when the time was right—and timing was everything in politics—made the leap to city council, next to State Assembly.

Then the big one. *And* reelection.

His convoy turned south on Trinity. Traffic backed up for a television shoot, a grip truck double-parked.

He was drawn to his reflection in the passenger window, noting the deep creases under the eyes, a few lines around the ears. Despite the stress of his office and frequent insomnia, his God-given handsomeness hadn't failed him yet. His biological mother and father might have been losers in life, but at least they left him with good genes. Movie-star looks and estimable adoptive parents who had given him the best education money could buy. He was fluent in Spanish. Portuguese was solid. He was everyman. Shot scratch golf and had a wicked first step on the basketball court. Talked with the command of an Ivy League debate champion but could yuck it up at the Southside precinct halls.

He was border patrol, banquet hall, *and* boardroom.

With His Honor, you never knew who—or what—you were talking to.

The Mayor closed his eyes and thought of kissing a girl, feeling her braces rough against his tongue, and then forcing her head underwater. The daydream was short-lived, however. His communications chief put a stack of note cards in his hand. Talking points for his speech at the breakfast jumped out at him. *Children. Workforce. Austere conditions. Sobering financial realities. Imprudence. Implications. Allegations.*

The girl in his momentary reveries was Maya—always Maya.

Ironic that he was on his way to address the State of the City, a chummy affair that constituted a lot of glad-handing and palm-greasing among members of the city council, the judiciary, and

an assortment of influential businessmen. Despite the buffet provided by a downtown hotel, the theater on display was enough to
induce nausea. Just a mob of latter-day feudal lords with their com-
peting interests, looking to milk as much profit as they could from a
metropolitan area already suffocating from dysfunction.

His Honor's city was a broken place, and the grift never ended.

There was a budget shortfall, and the sewer system on the
verge of collapse. High unemployment, the transportation net-
works in disrepair, crime on the rise, and the country at war. Plus
friction between the state and city governments, a billion dollars and counting in unfunded pension obligations. Allegations of
pay-to-play dealings and his procurement chief had just struck a
plea deal.

City cops had shot a ninety-year-old woman by accident, raiding
the wrong house in a drug bust.

Even the weather had been lousy.

But it was his job to spin this chaos into something hopeful.
Slap a happy face on what he knew to be the insidious beginnings
of outright collapse.

Sirens. Smoke. Starvation. Gunfire. The world reduced to rebar.
It didn't bother him a bit.

He mulled the upcoming speech, made some notes, and memorized the numbers of massaged crime statistics. A police helo buzzed
overhead. He glimpsed the gilded dome of the capitol building. The
tenets of his Justice Tower Initiative swirled like lyrics from a summer song he couldn't quite recall.

And Maya was never far away in his thoughts.

The first time he had her, that body in between adolescence and
womanhood.

A twinge of arousal forced itself against his underwear.

Every few seconds Eric Lambert glanced at him, as if he was adept at reading The Mayor's mind, considering what he found there to be agreeable.

His speech had been a success at the State of the City breakfast. Big applause. That familiar adrenaline high followed. It was a rush like no other, the performance part of politics as addictive for him as youthful flesh.

"*Governor,*" Lambert had whispered to him afterward.

"I do like the sound of that." They planned to announce the run soon.

The Mayor followed his director of security into City Hall, up the cream marble steps between balustrades four stories tall, the Gothic government building a twelve-story tower in the heart of town. It boasted pointed arches and uninterrupted piers, concrete reinforcement, the veneer a charcoal-colored terra-cotta. The lobby was bustling. The Mayor nodded. Smiled. Shook hands.

His Honor looked past pillars, toward the walls hung with oil paintings and portraits, his city in retrospect. They depicted schools desegregated. Color barriers broken. An assassination attempt on one of his predecessors.

The Mayor's offices occupied the entire top floor.

He had just come from a ribbon-cutting ceremony, dedicating a new park in Eastside. His afternoon schedule included a meeting with the city manager, incident reports, twenty-minute blocks with twenty different constituents. Pastors, architects, consultants, charity organizers, advocates of various homeowner associations.

"Time for lunch today?"

They were in His Honor's private quarters. Lambert checked his watch and shook his head.

"Can I?"

"You may," Lambert said and produced a bullet-shaped container from his coat pocket and handed it to The Mayor. He turned it upside down, twisted the tip until he heard a *click*. He held the bullet up to his nose and snorted. He repeated the process for the other nostril, handed the bullet back to Lambert. He nodded and sniffed again and then closed his eyes.

"Needed that."

Lambert smiled.

The Mayor got up and checked himself out in the lavatory mirror. Washed his hands. Straightened his tie. He sniffed a few times, color deepening in his face. Lambert parted curtains to allow more sunlight into the office, and then drifted to a corner, his back against a floor-to-ceiling bookshelf. Across the alleyway they heard the rhythmic ping of a construction crew.

There was a knock at the outer door. His secretary came in as he left the bathroom.

"How long are we going to have to put up with that racket?"

"Another year probably," she said. "Your two twenty and four o'clock canceled."

"Thank you, Eva. Paul on his way?"

"He is. With a wheelbarrow full of stimulus and citizen sat reports."

The Mayor waved her out and settled in behind his stately desk. He looked at the looming high-rise one block away, The Mayor admiring not the building's architecture so much as the numerous kickbacks resulting from its construction.

"Are they ever going to finish that damn thing?" he said.

He wiped his nose. Tapped a foot on the floor. Three neat stacks of papers demanded his attention. He scanned the top sheet in each stack, and then shook his head at Lambert.

"Tomorrow you'll be having dinner with the Chinese bankers," Lambert said.

"What was the matter with that blow? Can't keep my high."

Lambert nodded and offered him the bullet again. His Honor smiled, pleased with that reminder of his stature. He sniffed, handed the bullet back, and then ran a hand across his nose

"Keeping this high is like trying to hit a moving target."

Lambert waited, knowing what else was on his mind. "I haven't heard anything—about her."

"We didn't make a mistake, did we?"

"There was no other option."

"I miss her, Eric."

"I know you do. But I do wish the subject would vanish, like her."

"You don't think they hurt her, do you?"

"Weren't supposed to." Lambert paused.

The Mayor nodded, his eyes losing focus.

"Do you think I can get another?"

"I'll make the arrangements," Lambert said, not looking at him. "Any preference, sir?"

Lambert took a long breath.

"Nothing compares to Maya. It wasn't even the sex," he said. "You understand? She was like—like a kitten. A kitten I rescued from the street."

"It is what it is."

"But not her fault. I realize that now. It was—I was just a little careless. Like to hear myself talk a little too much. I don't think she was, you know, an informant. Do you?"

"No telling. But it had to be done."

"I won't be so loose-lipped with the next one."

"Lucio will need some time."

"Why? He's practically warehousing them. Just tell him I'll take anything for the time being. Long as they're soft and obedient."

Lambert hesitated, as if he wanted to demur.

"Lucio needs time—to be appropriately selective."

"Just make the damn call."

There was another knock at the office door. Eva again.

"Reps from the Metro Youth Foundation are here, sir."

The Mayor's face clouded as he switched gears, finding the proper tone of voice and demeanor for the visitors.

"Invite those sweethearts Rashida and Samuel in here," he said without missing a beat, loud enough so all could hear. "And fetch coffee and sandwiches from the deli. I'll have chicken salad on wheat. If I remember correctly, macaroni salad and cranberry juice for Miss Rashida and pastrami with extra mustard for Sammy. I do believe he likes those barbecue potato chips. Cream soda to drink. Eric?"

Lambert shook his head. He unbuttoned his blazer, revealing a tan belt slide gun holster, and took another seat in a leather chair in a far corner of the office.

The meetings ran late. They always did. The Mayor snorted his way through the afternoon before heading to a late supper at a celebrity chef's restaurant in Glenwood Park. His Honor enjoyed a private dining room. His chief of staff was there, with consultants from a company that did business with the city, an old pal from law school, an Atlanta-based film producer, an airport concessions lobbyist, and a television personality from Channel 2. Talk was plentiful but not cheap. News cycle was dominated by casualty reports, the bombings

in Baghdad, and locally by the murder of an undercover cop. There
was also the budget crisis, tax hikes, layoffs, complimentary playoff
tickets, a famous actor in town playing a superhero, sexual intrigue
of the city's social elite, college football, and a political cartoon on
yesterday's editorial page depicting The Mayor with silver spoons
for teeth, his smile exaggerated wide and mischievous, his pockets turned inside out as the mansion behind him was renovated by
workers wearing three-piece suits.

A skilled raconteur, The Mayor commanded the dinner party
with anecdotes, tailoring his speech and mannerisms for sophisti-
cated company. Wineglasses stayed full. Dinner was exceptional.
The chef came over for a photo op, a jolly bearded man covered in
tattoos. The Mayor had been operating at a high energy level for
fourteen hours straight.

Charming, eloquent, powerful.

And venal as a street con.

For optics he had voluntarily taken a pay cut, and funneled his
remaining salary to charity, a symbolic gesture as the budget crisis
deepened. He insisted on paying for dinner that evening but the
gesture was an empty one. All theater. The lobbyist for airport concessions had already made arrangements, charging the meal to a corporate credit card with 30 percent gratuity.

Later, almost midnight, The Mayor was chauffeured home to his
gated lakeside estate. On the ride he grew morose and withdrawn,
having hit the wall.

His house was on three acres. Six bedrooms, five baths, master
on main, terrace-level guest suites, a heated pool, full gym and basketball courts. Lambert reminded him of the next day's light load as
the car pulled into the circular drive. Recommended a workout for
His Honor. A midweek micro-detox.

A housekeeper opened the door.

The Mayor sat down at a grand piano in the salon and stared at the keys. He started to sob. Lambert stood by with his arms folded.

"I miss her daughterly wiles, Eric. We did that one, you know, the stepdaughter routine? The horny stepsister, the noisy neighbor. She loved playacting with me."

"What can I say?" Lambert said.

"Why did we do it?"

"You told her everything," Lambert said, and then calmly corrected with, "and Lucio's got her on tape with that narc. For our new friends in Matamoros, there was no other choice."

The Mayor nodded sullenly. The sound of the piano echoed through the house.

Lambert let himself out. The sport utility was waiting. He caught a ride back to a parking garage near City Hall. His day wasn't over. From his office he called an answering service. A few minutes later the secure phone rang. He got an address and a time.

Lambert drove toward Hartsfield-Jackson Airport, listening to talk radio, to the lonely souls out in the post-midnight void. Propagators, inciters, warmongers, barstool crackpots, and fiery personalities auguring ruin. He put the windows down. The air was warm and humid. He passed loiterers at crosswalks. Zombies milled outside a convenience store. There were low-burn flares in one intersection, broken glass glittering in a gutter, the aftermath of a collision waiting on an inbound siren.

Lambert heard more sirens as he drove past Grady Memorial Hospital. A Level 1 trauma center, surgeons some of the best in the country at treating multiple gunshot wounds.

They got plenty of practice.

On the radio a caller bickered with the host. The country was going to hell. It had been and always would be.

Near the airport he watched a 747 on twinkling approach. The city and its troubles were mostly behind him now.

He looked in the rearview and imagined the skyline on fire.

And knew the voices on the radio were right. *Straight to hell*, he thought.

He met Lucio in an industrial spur ten miles east of the airport. Lambert drove parallel to abandoned railroad tracks, gravel and debris crunching under the tires. Weeds grew from cracks in the asphalt. Old smokestacks were silhouetted against the sky under a harvest moon.

A stray dog rooted through garbage, shying away when the headlights caught its eyes.

He turned the car into the yard of an old ironworks foundry. Gang tags and graffiti covered the concrete façade with mere shards of glass in their window frames. Two Tahoes were parked near a loading dock. Lambert turned his sedan to face them. He left the engine running. Grimes got out of one of the cars, opened the back door for Lucio. They walked over, stopped three yards from Lambert, and looked him over. Eyeballed the holstered .45 at his hip but said nothing.

"Hands where I can see them," Grimes said. "We've got you covered."

Lambert noted a shooter lying low on the foundry's roofline.

"Seriously?"

"No offense, Fallujah," Lucio said. "Prefer to be tactically sound. What's this about?"

"He wants more teenage pussy."

"Big Brother wants another?" Lucio said. By moonlight Lambert noticed the greased forearm tattoo on the mend.

Lucio laughed.

"Can you get him another like Maya?"

"Not while the first one's still alive."

Lambert cocked his head in annoyance.

"Say again?"

"We ran into a problem. Girl didn't go down easy."

"What are you talking about? How'd she get away? She wasn't a goddamn black belt."

"Had help from a swamper with a twelve-gauge."

"Jesus Christ."

"Hey, Blackwelder, we're taking care of it."

"Oh, you think I was a mercenary? You've got no fucking idea what I am."

"We're all mercs, baby."

"So how do you know she's not sitting in custody somewhere? Singing for her supper."

"My girls don't talk."

"She did."

"Maya and that narc exchanged words, correct. Don't know if they met again. But Snakeskin understands that I am a serious person."

Lambert nodded.

"So where is the little bitch?"

Lucio's eyes went narrow as a lizard's.

"In our hearts and minds, war crimes. In our hearts and minds."

FIVE

THERE HAD BEEN NO SUPPER that night. Maya, feeling ill, crawled back into bed and slept through most of the following day. Leonard brought her water, soup stock with heavy cream, only to have it refused. She struggled through fits, terrors, jags of restless sleep, at one point wetting the bed. Talking to some invisible attacker in her nightmares.

"No-no-no! I won't do that!"

In the late hours Leonard sat down beside her. She mumbled and shook her head, distraught in her dreams, giving off a fever heat he felt when adjusting her blanket. He patted her back and sang an old hymn to her—"Pass Me Not, O Gentle Savior"—thinking about the abuse she had endured in her life.

Keeping secrets apparently that almost had got her killed.

Finally she calmed, and Leonard left her sleeping and fed the cats. Topping off bowls around the house's exterior with cornmeal and spoiled meat.

The following morning he took a turn around his place with the shotgun. He'd been down to the water to check his lines when he'd shot a five-pound swamp rabbit flushed from the cover of some stumps. Leonard went armed anytime he walked his property, almost eight hundred acres of remote bottomlands, timber lots, and pastures. There was a good meal everywhere he looked, a squirrel perched on a tree limb or game birds on the wing. The land denied him nothing.

He thought about the time as a child when he had suffered a protracted bout of grippe, almost died of it. When his appetite returned Leonard's mother had cooked a big rabbit pie, smothered down in thick flour gravy with plenty of black pepper and the notion struck Leonard that such a meal was exactly what Maya needed.

An hour before sunset he got to work in the kitchen. Leonard left the rabbit meat on the bone, tossed the pieces in a skillet with some butter. He added apple and onion, salt and pepper, a little bacon rind, cider, and stock. Brought it to a simmer and covered the pan.

He was kneading dough when he heard her call out to him from down the hall. Maya's voice sounded small and timid behind the bathroom door.

"That you, Leonard?"

He stood outside the door and knocked lightly.

"It's me. Good you're awake finally. How're you feeling?"

"I'm sick."

Leonard ran a hand across his stubbled chin.

"You want more aspirin? Some sassafras tea with whiskey might do the trick, too."

"Not sick *that* way. I need tampons," she said.

Leonard shrugged.

"You mean, like a sanitary pad?"

There was only silence and if Leonard could see through walls he would have observed Maya sitting on the toilet, staring between her legs, head shaking as she mouthed the words: *What the fuck?*

"No," she said, raising her voice. "Tampons. You know? Feminine hygiene products."

"Oh, okay," Leonard said.

"Super plus! Plastic applicators!"

"All right, all right."

He backed away from the door and began pacing the hall, glancing at the bathroom as if Maya would appear any second and announce her problem was solved. He thought of Marjean's belongings—dresses, perfume, brushes, undergarments. Nothing like what Maya was asking for. He looked out a nearby window, at shadows stretching across the yard.

"Guess I'll have to hustle over to the pharmacy," he said, mumbling to himself. "Rather drink day-old dishwater than go to town, but, well—"

Leonard moved Marjean to the rocking chair in the living room, facing a window that provided a vista of a grassy side yard, a large American holly in the middle of it. The green berries were halfway to red and cedar waxwings were gobbling them up like candy. He knelt beside the mannequin.

"Marjean, only one thing to do, right? Got to do this."

He waited and stared at Marjean as if listening intently to a reply.

"She ain't sick and needin' a doctor, is she?"

Another moment passed. He took the mannequin's hand in his.

"All right, then," Leonard said. "But you're coming with me."

He tiptoed to the bathroom door, making sure to clear his throat and announce his nearness.

"Maya?" he said. "We're going. Speak now you need anything else."

"Just remember—tampons," she said. "And some clothes."

"Clothes?"

"Yeah, sweatpants, tank tops. Blue jeans. Underwear. Socks. Anything. Oh—and some shoes."

"Shoes."

"And a hairbrush. I'll pay you back. Promise."

"How you going do that?"

"I have ways," she said.

Leonard thought about her answer.

"Hell, I got plenty of money. Let me get a pen."

He scribbled down her requests. Shoe size. Pant size.

A moment later he heard bathwater running and backed away from the door.

Leonard carried Marjean out to the Studebaker. It had once been one of his old liquor cars back when Trickum was a dry county, the fastest in his fleet, with sandbags in the trunk so the vehicle would sit right. Too fond of the Studebaker to ever part with it, Leonard never stopped tinkering under the hood.

He made sure the mannequin was secure in the passenger seat before cranking the motor. He lit Marjean a cigarette, put it in the ashtray before lighting his own. His nerves were jangly. Leonard hated town, both in the abstract and as a reality. There were *people* in town.

Other people.

But there were also necessities that no girl could be without, and Maya needed his help.

He dropped the clutch and floored the gas, following tire marks into the sunset, a wake of sand and dust billowing after the Studebaker as he headed toward the firebreaks.

Leonard took the old logging road and passed from his property across state lands and after a mile or so he hit asphalt and drove north toward Trickum. On the outskirts of town he saw the dollar store, a gas station, and some houses and then crossed the train tracks for the Norfolk Southern. He turned toward Main and drove down a street lined with vacant buildings engulfed in kudzu, row houses, and ancient live oaks with their limbs draped in Spanish moss, the only shade to an otherwise listless grid of poverty. Men clustered on a stoop turned their heads and watched Leonard drive by. None waved in greeting. When he looked at them, they all averted their gaze. Dogs roamed freely. A woman carrying grocery bags stopped to stare at the Studebaker, as did the child at her side.

Two young boys rounded a corner on their bicycles and weaved behind Leonard's antique car, following, pointing, gawking, the boys' laughter high-pitched, malicious to his ears.

"Whoopee!" one of them said.

"Craaaaazy Leonard! Sticks his dong in a mannequin!"

This went on for several blocks, through four-way stops, the mini-parade drawing attention from pedestrians and porch-dwellers until Leonard abruptly stopped the car, causing the bikers to swerve to avoid the Studebaker's rear bumper. The bikes skidded and swung around, the riders glancing back at Leonard, their enthusiasm for pursuit waning. He held them with a glare that couldn't be taught, the stuff of legend, a look known all over the county, which had frozen everyone from the preacher's wife to revenue men to the pickled livers at the Owl's Roost where he did much of his business.

Leonard rolled down his window and motioned to the boys with his finger. They didn't dare move and stared dumbly at him.

"You know who I am?"

The older boy nodded.

"Then you know I'm mean enough to kill Jesus," Leonard said. "And don't you forget it."

Ronelle was filling a prescription for Maude Felty's blood pressure medication when she looked up and saw Leonard's Studebaker rumble into the pharmacy's parking lot. Maude turned and lifted her chin as if to see through the glasses resting on the bulb of her nose.

"My goodness," she said. "Done left the funny farm for a trip to town."

"That man scares the blazes out of me," Ronelle said.

She watched as Leonard got out, walked around and leaned over the passenger-side window of the Studebaker, presumably speaking to his mannequin.

"Oh, he's harmless as a rattlesnake."

"Whatever happened to his wife?"

Maude shrugged.

"Lot of gossip. Nobody knows. Wonder if he still got them stills on his land."

"Stills?"

"White lightning, sweetie. Man made a peach moonshine that was to die for. Keep a few jars from the old days in the cabinet for special occasions."

Ronelle handed the woman her medication and wished her a pleasant evening. Maude Felty hobbled toward the entrance, where she saw Leonard patiently holding the door. Ronelle couldn't understand for the life of her why the crazy ones waited till almost closing time to come by, as if there were a conspiracy all the town's deranged had cooked up.

"Evening, Maudy," Leonard said, tipping the brim of his straw hat.

"Evening, Leonard. You are looking right fit these days. How's that Marjean?"

"Ain't lost her looks and she's sweeter than angel cake."

"You give her my regards now."

Maude smiled gamely. Leonard nodded and walked into the pharmacy.

Ronelle watched him from the counter, recalling the stories about him that Maude Felty had alluded to, which were near mythic in the town. Leonard had been a notorious bootlegger, rumor of a fortune buried as deep as graves he'd dug for those foolish enough to trespass on his property. Ronelle remembered a story she once heard, that Leonard had spiked whiskey with ipecac and sold it to all his debtors, an event her grandmother referred to as the night when vomit flowed through the streets of Trickum.

Other stories about Leonard were grimmer, scary to adolescents. Hearsay that he killed his wife and ate her. Or that she killed herself, and the pain proved too much for Leonard to bear, so he took him a mannequin as a replacement and acted as if nothing had happened. Or that his land was haunted by the ghosts of all the children he had kidnapped and tortured, and if you didn't behave, ol' man Leonard was going to string you up and dress you like a pig, prop up your bones in his field with all the other scarecrows.

Not too long ago, during her senior year of high school, Ronelle had been loitering outside the movie theater with some friends when Leonard cruised by in a LaSalle coupe, that mannequin as usual in the passenger's seat. It wasn't uncommon back then to see Leonard and *Marjean* at the pictures. He even bought the mannequin popcorn, the manager always happy to charge him for two adults. Before the ridicule or gossip became too much, Ronelle figured, or Leonard's contempt for the outside world diminished his interest in participating in it. Ronelle's boyfriend at the time, a varsity linemen named Johnny Powell, was a cocksure farm boy from the next town over. Johnny hadn't heard the stories about Leonard or the unspoken rule that you never ever talked to him.

That night at the movie theater, Johnny Powell had taken exception to the leisurely passes Leonard made in that LaSalle, possibly thinking the old man was ogling the girls, and yelled his displeasure at Leonard.

On his next appearance Leonard stopped the car and got out.

Everyone reacted as if a cougar had just been dropped off curbside, save for Ronelle's knuckleheaded boyfriend. He flicked away a cigarette and stuck out his chest.

Leonard's eyes were a deadly shade of gray and wild with hate. He stopped a foot from Johnny and sniffed.

"Put your hands on me, mister. I dare you," Johnny said.

But Leonard's expression never changed. There was a chilling intensity about him when he said, "When the old Master draws your number and calls you, son, it'll be *my* face you see last."

Johnny flinched, unable to speak as Leonard got back into the LaSalle and drove off. Johnny wasn't quite right ever after that exchange, either, as if the encounter with a very capable and cruel man had crippled his ego permanently. And all it took were some words and a look.

The face Leonard showed Johnny Powell hadn't changed much over the years, Ronelle thought. He was older, sure, but probably no less lethal and from what she could see for herself no less crazy.

Leonard produced a list from the bib pocket of his overalls and made his way down the nearest aisle, pausing to study a bottle of shampoo, a toothbrush, some paste. He went up the next aisle, studying the piece of paper in his hand, a sustained grimace on his face. Finally he looked up, acknowledged Ronelle, and approached the counter.

"Evening," he said.

"Evening. Something I can help you with?"

Leonard squared his shoulders as if anticipating a difficulty.

"I need some uh, super plus," he said.

Ronelle resisted a laugh. "Pardon me?"

Leonard looked down at his list again.

"For a woman's monthly."

"Oh, my," she said and pointed. "You'll find hygiene products in aisle five."

Leonard nodded tensely, located the appropriate aisle, scratching his jaw, his eyes going to the list then back to the shelves. He stood there a while. Ronelle couldn't take her eyes off him. Finally he called out to her.

"Which ones would you recommend?"

"Those right there where your hand is. Box with the green stripe. Those are the ones I use."

Leonard bought the tampons, along with some toiletries, paying out of an old leather billfold. She handed Leonard his change and trailed him to the front entrance, wishing him a good night, ready to lock the doors before a clown car skidded up, spilling out circus freaks.

But Leonard didn't return to the Studebaker. He headed for the discount clothing store across the street.

It was right about the time Ronelle's brother-in-law pulled up in his patrol car. Leonard glanced in the direction of Jack Chalmers, and then walked off with an aura of weary forbearance. Chalmers stared at him, the sight of Leonard made all the more curious by the drugstore bag he clutched protectively in his right hand.

Ronelle balanced the cash register and began to lock up.

Chalmers, his shift over, leaned against a mirrored column, flipping through the pages of the latest *Field & Stream*.

"So what was Leonard doing here?" he said.

"Maybe he's got him a new girlfriend," Ronelle said.

The Studebaker's engine cranked in the parking lot and reared to a growl. Chalmers watched through the window as it pulled away.

"Can't speak for his mannequin, but he keeps that old Commander in right smart condition."

"He still make his own whiskey?"

"Probably not. But I heard at one time he had moonshine buried all over the county. What was he buying?"

"Tampons."

"Very funny."

"Serious as a heart attack. Three boxes of ultra absorbent. Plus some other things. Then walked himself straight over to the Clothing Carousel. Makes no sense. He doesn't have family, right?"

Chalmers didn't answer. A perplexed look had entered his eyes.

"You about to finish up here?"

"Another minute. Is it true his wife tore his back to shreds with a scattergun? Or that he killed her? Heard so many stories growing up."

"She was for sure the temperamental type," Chalmers said. "Or so I heard."

"Ain't it true you're kin to some Moyes from way back?"

Chalmers didn't answer, and by the look on his face it was clear the question was unwanted. Ronelle came out from the prescriptions counter with her purse, store smock rolled up under one arm.

"Forget I asked," she said. "Thanks for the ride."

"What family's for. You got that acne cream for Cale?"

"Right here."

She handed him the ointment and glanced at the wall clock in sundries.

"Let's make time. You mind dropping me at the Busy Bee?"

"Got a date?"

"Just drinks with someone."

"Like he doesn't have a name?"

"Yeah. Just plain old *someone*."

On the way to his cruiser Chalmers pondered Ronelle's lack of ambition and attitude of sulky impertinence. Weekends his sister-in-law had been coming home very late, or not at all. Spent Saturdays sobering up before doing it all over again. His wife was worried sick of course, but Ronelle always insisted on paying a share of the rent, and never showed up with a man for Chalmers to deal with. The one rule Chalmers made clear when she had moved in with him and Kelly Anne. Otherwise he didn't try to present himself as any kind of authority figure or offer any kind of brotherly advice. She wasn't about to listen to anybody's counsel. So they tolerated each other, and as for the provocative looks he sometimes got from her, Chalmers let it go by.

The Busy Bee Bar & Grille was a stand-alone trailer by the river that catered to Trickum's young and restless with cheap beer and live music. There was a roofed patio with a string of American flags tacked along the frame. Slips on the river accommodated the transient houseboat crowd. Under a previous owner the Bee had once been a great place to eat, a fish camp famous for shellcrackers fried in deep fat. Now the place inspired nothing but unwanted pregnancies and fistfights, although at least once or twice a year those fists were replaced with pistols.

"You be careful in there," Chalmers said.

"I'm in good hands."

Ronelle winked and got out of the patrol car. She lit a cigarette and walked across the mostly empty parking lot, a scrim of smoke trailing her.

Chalmers watched her to the entrance and then wheeled his cruiser out of the parking lot, noting the look of rain in the sky but not wanting to go home just yet. Leonard's tract wasn't far if he remembered correctly. Only slightly out of the way. He felt compelled to take a ride, jarred by memories stirred up like silt from the bottom of a pond.

He drove between fields of cotton, mullet, soybeans and peanuts, the big strippers and pickers out there fresh from maintenance and ready for a harvest. Agribusiness conglomerates owned most of the farms in the county, with only a few old-timers still holding on to their land, lives both rooted to the properties and trapped by them. Some of the farmers took on loans they knew they couldn't afford or got involved with grants and bought themselves swimming pools and cable television and brand-new pickup trucks instead of investing in equipment or repairs. Raised a few towns over by an aunt and uncle on his mother's side, Chalmers was glad his uncle hadn't been a farmer, avoided the heartache and debt his friends accumulated in lifetimes robbing Peter to pay Paul under the unforgiving sun.

He thought about Leonard again, recalled the rumors, apocryphal or not, escapades from a rebellious, freewheeling youth. Precarious dealings that could cause a man to lose his nerve, end up old and played out before his time. But Chalmers knew it wasn't moonshine that made Leonard crazy.

Marjean.

How could they?

Chalmers passed one of two wildlife management areas in the county, ten thousand acres full of quail and turkey and deer. Near the river he saw signs for boat landings, a favorite fishing hole of his near the lake. There was little traffic. He waved to the driver of a SUV, bass boat in tow, and then came upon an armadillo in the road. Chalmers skirted the animal, drifting across the dotted line, knowing they had a talent with one jump of making a mess of a car's undercarriage.

He sighted the radio tower and slowed, not entirely sure which road to turn on. Chalmers saw an abandoned home, satellite dish in the yard, long in disrepair and seemingly held in place by kudzu. There were mailboxes on the opposite shoulder of the road, a narrow dirt drive, but no residences in view.

Chalmers took the next right just as rain dotted the windshield of his Crown Vic.

The clay road was stitched with tread marks, canopied by oaks draped with Spanish moss, wild blackberry growing so close he could have rolled down the window and picked a handful. He knew Leonard lived between the paper company and state-managed game lands, a homestead bordered to one side by a swamp and on all others by big timber. Hard to get to if you didn't know which roads to take, most of them hardpan, rutted, spooky one-tracks that led deep into the woods. God forbid he got stuck out there in a rainstorm.

The sky darkened. Chalmers stopped and looked down a fire-break, glimpsed a sounder of hogs disappear into the brush. How long had it been, he thought, since he had been out that way? He'd been a kid, but that's all he knew for certain.

Prompted by thunder and wary of rain, Chalmers turned his cruiser back toward pavement. By the time he hit the highway, the sky had opened. He drove home, ill at ease, nagged by the sight of Leonard Moye, as if a confluence of events was forming around him, its significance yet to be revealed.

The Busy Bee was more crowded than usual, every chair at the bar occupied by some all-day drunks, other folks looking to get in off the lake and out of the rain, men on their way home from work needing a couple pops before facing nagging wives or the loneliness of an unmade bed. An old river rat circled the room's lone pool table, painter's jeans and boat shoes, skin sun-crisped, tattoo sagging on one skinny forearm, his tank top revealing a pelt's worth of chest hair. It was a dingy scene, the overhead fluorescents dimmed by cigarette smoke. A muted television behind the bar gave glimpses of news from overseas, none of it good, but nobody paid much attention.

Ronelle found an open booth. Lit another cigarette and ordered a beer. She watched the rain. A DJ arrived, soaked, lamenting wet equipment. By nightfall a livelier crowd began to trickle in, drawn by Hank Williams Jr. and the two-for-one specials, chicken fingers and fried catfish. Folks with dopers' eyes, popping Oxycontin like breath mints.

It was near eight o'clock when she heard a chassis-rattling sub-woofer outside. The rain and low thunder couldn't drown out Kevin Chukes's car stereo in the parking lot.

Nobody paid much attention when Kevin slid into Ronelle's booth, Styrofoam cup in hand. She leaned across the table to kiss him on the cheek.

"What's good?"

"Nothing, sugar. How are you?" she said.

Kevin grinned and ordered a beer but didn't touch it, sneaking sips of the mysterious purple liquid in the to-go cup he had brought with him. He had the sagging build of an All-American fullback gone soft. In fact he had been a high school football star whose lack of common sense had got him kicked off the Seminoles in Tallahassee a few years back. Lessons unlearned. Ronelle knew that Kevin was currently driving on a suspended license, often in possession of a controlled substance, and sleeping with the sister-in-law of a Trickum County deputy sheriff.

Ronelle and Kevin agreed to split some hot wings.

For a while neither of them spoke, Ronelle sneaking glances at her beau of just a few weeks while he watched two anglers shoot a game of nine ball. A few people he knew and a few he didn't came by the booth to chat, Kevin posturing with what cool he had left in a county that revered its athletes. One even asked for an autograph and a photo. He obliged. Ronelle smiled desirably at him. He wore his hair in a bleached blond Caesar cut, heavy-lidded eyes with a ring through one brow, a head perpetually bobbing to music only he apparently heard.

She guessed he was high on codeine cough syrup, codeine she had been supplying from the pharmacy. He preferred to mix it with hard candy and lemon-flavored soda. The action at the billiard table couldn't hold his interest, and he was forced to finally look at Ronelle. When he spoke she noticed his tongue, stained purple as a bruise.

"Got that shit you wanted," he said.

She gave him an expectant look.

Kevin slipped a hand into the pocket of his letterman's jacket, which he wore year-round, then passed a baggie to Ronelle under the table. She glanced down and tucked it in her purse.

"And what have you got there?" she said, reaching for the Styrofoam in his other hand.

He pulled the cup away.

"Uh-uh. Last batch. I'm about out."

He fixed her with a pleading look.

"Unless you can help me?"

Since the ninth grade Kevin had been a heartbreaker with a bad boy rep, and Ronelle was far from immune. Still remembered for his 105-yard return against West End in the state playoffs, now he spent most of his time laying down tracks for various underground mixtapes, always talk of a big record deal that never materialized. He earned studio time by selling marijuana and ecstasy to teenagers out of his customized Oldsmobile. Codeine was a new enterprise, and Ronelle wasn't naïve as to the reason for his interest in her. He had shown her a sweet side, however.

Ronelle bit her lip. A flashback of him taking her from behind, and the resultant orgasm, had her quadriceps quivering. Kevin had been pestering her for weeks to supply him more codeine from the pharmacy. Said he could make bank with it up in Albany and Columbus. And he would cut her in. Kevin told her repeatedly it was a "sellers' market," as if he had heard the phrase on television and fallen in love with its economic sophistication.

Funny how life was, Ronelle thought. Borderline alcoholic and now buying weed from a once-promising football star turned college dropout turned low-level dealer. Who in all likelihood was courting her just to score prescription cough syrup? Kevin of all people.

"I'll do it," she eventually said. "Just give me some time."

Kevin smiled. He reached under the table and squeezed her thigh. Ronelle shuddered.

"One more thing," he said. "Got a cousin from A-Town. Called me up, asking about some crazy old man lives out in the woods. Said he got him a field with scarecrows?"

"Must be talking about Leonard," Ronelle said. "Now that is a coincidence. Came into the drugstore tonight."

"So you know where he lives at?"

"Sort of. I could ask Jack. He'd know, although it's kind of a touchy subject for some reason. Why?"

"My cousin said something about a real estate deal, looking to buy land from him but nobody can get hold of the guy or figure how to get to his place. Might be a little money in it for us. Like a finder's fee."

"See what I can do. Meanwhile, what are *you* going to give me for it?"

She reached under the table and grabbed the crotch of his jeans.

"What you can't get enough of," Kevin said.

"Oh, yeah?"

"You my girl?"

She blushed, too smitten to admit she knew better than to answer *yes*.

Chalmers was five minutes from the house when dispatch found him.

"Unit Five, what's your 20?"

He answered the call.

"Got a 10-50, Jack. Need you to do the notification."

"Copy that," Chalmers said, then clicked off, acknowledging the code for an accident fatality with a choice swear before keying his radio. "Guess I won't be eating a hot meal anytime soon."

"Sorry, Jack."

"Summerlin not available?"

"Negative. He's 10-6."

Busy my ass, Chalmers thought. Dispatch relayed the victim's name and address. Teletype verification. An electrician on his way home from work had been hit head-on by a doublecab hauling a landscaping trailer.

The residence was off the highway, near an easement used by the power company. Chalmers knew a shortcut, an access road that took him right past his favorite fishing spot; the bite good there early in the morning, top water and grass beds being the best bet for bass. The landing was empty, however. Black gum trees swayed in the wind as rainwater washed away all the bird shit from the ramp, big drops thrumming against the mass of lily pads near the shoreline.

The newly paved road wrapped around the pond and merged with another road. Chalmers hung a right. Realtor signs lined the grassy shoulder like gawkers on a parade route. He passed a partially full development, modular homes for the most part well maintained. Some units had flower beds out front, or an aboveground swimming pool. Chalmers found the address. The rain began to let up, but it didn't matter. He spotted toys in the front yard. A swing set.

Fuck me, he thought.

Notifications were the worst part of the job. Chalmers was usually met by a blank look. Followed by a whimper, a solemn shake of the head, other times a grieving wail. Some people were incredulous; shocked into disbelief, yet others had an eagerness to know more, no matter how painful the details. One man, upon hearing his son had been killed in a drunk-driving accident, passed out in the dooryard of his home, landing facedown in a pile of dog shit. Chalmers learned then that you got the next of kin seated before you dropped the news.

No matter how many times he rehearsed his speech, Chalmers was always aware at that moment life's senseless cruelties had a face—*his.*

A small boy answered the door. Chalmers heard other children inside, the sound of a television. Smelled dinner cooking. The boy just stared at him.

"Hey, son. Is your mother home?"

The boy nodded, held up a hand for Chalmers to wait on the little porch, and disappeared inside. Chalmers heard a clatter of pots and pans, then a woman's complaining voice.

She was thin and pretty. Neatly dressed. Her face clouded when she saw him.

"Can I help you?"

Chalmers removed his campaign hat and turned it in his hands.

"Cyrene Dobson?"

"Yes?"

"Can we speak inside?"

They sat down in the living room. Chalmers sat opposite the newly widowed woman, noting that despite the havoc children usually caused, the trailer was spotless. There was a framed portrait of Jesus on the wall behind the sofa. Experience taught him religious made for serious melodrama.

Chalmers steeled himself.

"I'm here about your husband," he said. "Wallace was involved in a traffic accident earlier this evening. He did not survive the collision."

A moment passed between them. Chalmers expected waterworks, waiting for that shade of despair to pass over her eyes, and was about to add that Wallace's death was instantaneous, that he hadn't suffered, but Cyrene Dobson inexplicably smiled. What she said next chilled him bone-deep.

"I know. Jesus visited me this morning and told me it was Wallace's time."

Before Chalmers could respond, she said, "Children. Gather around now. Mama wants to tell you something."

"Now I'm not sure that's such a good idea," Chalmers said. She raised a finger and hushed him. He was shocked by the woman's eerie calmness, the serenity with which she had accepted the news. It defied denial.

The children, three in all, crowded their mother on the couch. All close in age, the mood of the two boys and one girl was downright cheerful. Chalmers was speechless.

"Children," Dobson said. "Remember how I told you your father had taken a vow with me, and that one day he would join Jesus in heaven? *Today* your father went to Jesus. Now is the time to rejoice."

Chalmers regarded the family, thinking he might be the one to cry. She looked from her children to the deputy, and then extended a hand across the coffee table. He took it wordlessly. Without any prompting, the children joined hands and bowed their heads.

"Are you a spiritual man, Officer?"

He shook his head, not sure it a sufficient answer.

"You've suffered heartache in your life, haven't you? And something today has reminded you of some old wounds long forgotten."

"How did—? Yes, I have. But—"

"Pray with us then, will you?"

Chalmers thought about Leonard Moye.

He closed his eyes and listened.

They were in a conference room at City Hall East.

The Mayor sat patiently while a makeup artist from the local affiliate prepped him for his interview. The news anchor sat opposite him, legal pad in his lap, face thoroughly bronzed and ready for prime time. There was a discussion already underway, not about the war or murdered narcotics officer or budget deficits, but cures for tennis elbow.

Sammy Kemp, The Mayor's media relations officer, offered Lambert a rare smile. Her mood was dour, however, as chatter about a spate of shootings and the dead cop dominated recent headlines. She shook her head in disgust.

"There a problem?" Lambert said.

"Blowback. Our police chief is an idiot and shouldn't be allowed in front of a microphone."

"Never let a crisis go to waste, right?"

Kemp looked him over.

"It's weird."

"What is?"

"How you focus on him every few seconds."

"What?"

"Your eyes," she said, and gestured to The Mayor. "They find him like a compass needle finding true north."

"I'll take that as a compliment."

"Are all you former Blackwelder guys like that?"

"Like what?"

"So goddamn creepy."

Lambert had already run half a dozen scenarios since the news crew had arrived, calculating his response to an assassination attempt, bomb threat, fire, and medical emergency. He watched a grip make some tweaks to the lighting grid. The segment's producer pointed at his watch and circled a finger in the air. Five minutes. The Mayor moistened his lips, uncrossed his legs, his light exchange with the news anchor over. Kemp went over to share a word in private with The Mayor. A moment later she joined Lambert behind the camera. An edgy silence followed.

"All hell is breaking loose."

"What is it?"

"Dirty cop gets a tip about a prostitution ring. Then gets murdered. Nobody knows anything. Feds might get involved. Boys in blue are closing ranks, covering their ass and the press is going nuts. The Mayor doesn't need another scandal like this."

"He needs it. He thrives on chaos," Lambert said, just loud enough for her to hear.

"Excuse me?"

"Chaos."

"Primary next November will be chaos. If he wants to win the governorship he better put a few fires out."

"He loves playing with fire."

"What?"

But Lambert didn't answer. The televised interview was about to begin.

The motel had had no vacancies. It never did.

The building was L-shaped, single-story, with a hail-damaged roof and lack of paint. In every room the curtains were drawn. Blending into the blight, the parking lot was intentionally kept dark, not enough light shining in the office to draw a moth. The neighborhood, if you could call it that, was notorious for crime scene tape, strewn across sidewalks like confetti after a parade. Detectives in the Crimes Against Persons squad had become so sick of working the area that they had once authored a *street memo* as a joke, proposing that the gangs take their war games to a more hospitable part of town.

An apartment complex next to the motel stood skeletal after fire, the remains neither demolished nor rebuilt. Girls and boys worked the street. One even conducted business from the comforts of a portable toilet. Bottom-of-the-barrel drug deals were the other economic reality, undisturbed by the occasional gunfire or the backwash of a patrolling helicopter.

Three blocks south there was a functioning strip mall with a heavily guarded liquor store and check-cashing facilities.

Lucio owned both.

As he did the girl in the motel's basement.

Grimes monitored a scanner, bouncing between frequencies, the silence broken by 10-codes and the voice of a dispatcher. Another of Lucio's employees watched everything with the minimal interest of a court stenographer.

Lucio squatted near the heavy-duty dog crate. Gestured with a finger to William Watkins.

William undid the hasp and opened the door. Reached inside and yanked the hood from the girl's head.

She looked around, blinking, her eyes as swollen as feeding ticks. Too exhausted to cry or scream. There were untouched crackers on the floor of the cage. A bedpan. Food and water bowls. Lucio licked his lips, studying the girl for signs of total submission, a broken spirit. He had been working on her for two weeks after she was snatched from a street corner in Overtown, Miami, then gagged, crated, and driven in a cargo van up Interstate 75 for delivery to a safe house in the West End, then to the motel basement. Disoriented in her passage by doses of "Georgia Home Boy," a nickname for the tranquilizer gamma hydroxybutyrate.

"You recognize my voice?" Lucio said.

"I think so."

"Am I your *Daddy?*"

She nodded.

"There wasn't a life before this one, now was there?"

She shook her head. A string of saliva hung from one corner of the girl's mouth.

"I know you got a grandmamma named Rosalee. I know you got a little sister and an older brother and a biologic in jail. And I can get to *all* of them."

The girl could barely keep her head up. Lucio reached out and raised her chin, gentle as lifting a stylus on a turntable.

"That's why you won't ever talk without my permission, baby girl. Because if you don't do what I say, I'll wipe your family off the face of the earth. Like they never existed."

He caressed the girl's cheek, holding her with his eyes.

"Now this has been the hard part, but Daddy wants to make it all better. Fix you up with new clothes, some jewelry, and nice-smelling perfume. Wash that stink off. From now on your name is *Coco*. You hear me?"

"*Coco*," she said hoarsely.

Lucio favored her with a smile, then looked back and jerked his head, a signal for Watkins and Grimes to prep the newly christened Coco for transportation to the next and final stop on her indoctrination tour—the massage parlor—where for the next week or so she would be pampered, amphetamized, fed, and manicured.

Soon after she would entertain her first client.

Currently on the eleven o'clock news.

Twenty minutes later, Lucio spoke to Grimes from the back seat of a Land Rover.

"When do you leave?"

"Tomorrow. William's cousin came through. Swamper's name is Leonard—Leonard Moye. We know exactly where he lives."

"Have everything you need?"

Grimes nodded.

"It's imperative she doesn't see sundown."

"Dinner for two."

"Make it three while you're sightseeing. William's done outlived his usefulness."

Grimes showed gold teeth in the mirror. Lucio's attention shifted to the sodium-lit street corners, reckoning the whores who worked the block. He felt a knot in his gut, a rare twist of anxiety. Only the thought of bodies floating facedown in a backwoods pond soothed his discomfort.

SIX

IT WAS DARK AND DRIZZLING when Leonard pulled into the barn, having driven through rain showers on the way back from town. The Studebaker's wheel wells were caked with mud. He reached for the shopping bags in Marjean's lap, recalling the looks he had received inside the clothing store while browsing the ladies' garments, and then he hustled on to the house.

He hadn't paid attention to designs or styles, but if Maya didn't care for what he bought, he figured, well, she could return them herself.

With Marjean upright in one arm, he was surprised when he walked in to find Maya sitting at the kitchen table, wearing one of his wife's robes, jittery as she smoked a cigarette. Leonard pitched the pharmacy bag on the table. Maya rose quickly, took a box of tampons and hurried down the hall to the bathroom.

Maya looked calmer when she reappeared a few minutes later. She sat down and crossed her legs. A small foot jumping nervously as she looked through the contents of the shopping bag from Clothing Carousel. She held up a plaid blouse and rolled her eyes. Then came sweatpants. Tank tops. Socks. A sweater with a snowman stitched on the front. Acid-washed blue jeans.

"Well—thanks, Leonard. They'll do."

He nodded with some relief and began rolling dough on a cutting board.

"Marjean say you could wear her bathrobe?"

The robe had a yellow tartan pattern, shoulder pads, a shawl collar, and wide-cut sleeves. It smelled of long-stale storage. It hung on Maya's slight frame and left little to the imagination with a glimpse of cleavage. Maya was accustomed to the look in men's eyes when they saw skin, but Leonard had no such reaction.

"Well," Maya said, fumbling for an answer. "Yes. She told me it'd be all right."

"Good," he said, apparently not concerned about Maya rooting through the closet in his bedroom. He went back to work kneading dough. "How's the fit of them shoes?"

She slipped into a white tennis sneaker without untying it.

"You must of thought I got clown feet?"

Leonard pitched a rag from the counter to Maya.

"Wad some of that up and stuff it in the toe. All it takes, girl, is a little *make do*."

Maya grinned, showing Leonard a remarkably straight set of white teeth marred only by a chipped incisor. A cut on the mend was crusty at one corner of her mouth. She had washed and brushed her hair, bound it with a thick rubber band. The skin of her arms was still badly scratched, but bathing had given her an unexpectedly healthy glow.

Maya eyed the stovetop, where Leonard was covering his stew with strips of piecrust.

"What's for dinner?" she said.

"Potpie. You ever got anything else to say?"

"I'm hungry, that's all," Maya said sulkily.

"Reckon might be my last earthly purpose to get some meat on your bones."

Maya drew another cigarette from the pack on the table. Leonard, watching her out of the corner of an eye, patted his pockets until he found the menthols he had bought in town. He handed them over.

"Before you smoke up all a mine," he said.

"Thanks."

Maya looked out the window, prompted by a renewed patter of rain on the roof. A cat sat on a porch railing cleaning itself.

"You know, it's not so bad here," she said.

"Compared to what else?"

"Everything else."

Leonard put the pie in the oven. Wiped his hands on the front of his jeans. He settled into the chair to the left of the mannequin. Her wig was canted to one side. Leonard carefully straightened it for her. Maya was inscrutable, smoking, watching.

"Find it to your liking, you're welcome to stay a while," he said.

"Can I ask you something?"

"Sure."

"Why do you give a damn about me?"

There was a tremor in her voice, a little bit of heartache catching a ride on her last word.

Leonard lit a cigarette and seemed to mull the question by swiping his tongue across his teeth. He looked over at the mannequin.

"Why don't you ask Marjean? Sitting there in her robe like the two of you became the best of friends."

Maya's chin came up. She stood and shucked the robe and tossed it across a vacant chair and faced him, trembling, naked except for the bit of tampon string between her thighs.

Leonard looked at her with no change of expression.

"Best you get in your new clothes now."

"Why don't you take me? All you got on your mind anyhow."

Leonard shook his head.

"No. Won't be none of that."

"Think you're too old? I can show you different, real fast."

"I said to dress yourself."

Leonard got up, turned his chair around to face the window. He sat down to smoke and watch the rain.

Maya dressed, putting on the sweat pants and tank top. She took a seat and cleared her throat. Leonard turned his head.

"I may be quick on the trigger with outlaw tendencies," he said. "But I never disrespected or took advantage of a woman in my life. You can ask Marjean."

He got up and walked to the oven and checked the potpie. Then he turned around and looked at Maya.

"What?" Maya said.

"Apologize to Marjean for your actions, girl."

After a couple of looks at the mannequin, Maya said, "I'm sorry. I didn't mean nothing. It's just—"

"Your way?"

"Yeah," Maya said grimly. "Only way of doing things I know of."

After a second Leonard nodded as if he understood. Maya watched him put a comforting hand on the mannequin's shoulder. She had seen weirdness in a variety of forms, and her first rule was never to ask. Pretend that some perversion was normal long enough, and pretty soon it *was* normal.

They regarded one another for a moment, and Leonard sighed and looked as though he was trying to muster the courage to ask her something unpleasant.

"Just what did fetch you up here?"

"Better if you don't know, Leonard."

"Only rule in this house is to shoot straight. Tell me."

"Okay," she said. "About two or three months ago a man hired one of the other girls, became kind of a regular, you know? Throwing parties, getting in good with the crew. Claimed to be a record producer and club promoter but turned out he was actually undercover. One night he asked me a few questions about the man I worked for."

"What kind of questions?" Leonard said.

"The kind you don't ask."

"Then what happened?"

Maya closed her eyes and shook her head.

"Two weeks later that cop turned up dead, and I woke up in the trunk of a car down here. Basically, it was like I was trash and he said to take it out."

"Who's *he*?"

"His name is Lucio. But all the girls call him *Daddy*."

"And you were made to give yourself to men for Lucio's profit? We're talking prostitution?"

Maya nodded.

Leonard let out a long breath.

"How on earth did that happen?" he said.

"My mother used to work a corner to make a couple dollars. But she was real bad on drugs and sold me off when I was twelve. Snatched me up in the middle of the night and handed me over to some guys. Kind of thing happens all the time."

Leonard was stoic, just listening, but his normally chilling gray eyes had softened, as if in sympathy for a badly wounded animal. He drew silently on a cigarette and blew the smoke from his nose.

"Where did they take you?" he said.

"They drove me and some other girls away. Part of the deal is they keep you pretty fucked up so you don't know where you're at or what day it is. Then I met Lucio. He took a liking to me right away."

She looked down, picked at a scab on one of her knuckles.

"Feels like I've been dreaming the past couple years. But it wasn't always bad. He bought us clothes, jewelry, put on these parties at a rich guy's house—a mansion. We would strut our stuff like fashion models, and they would use laser pointers on who they liked, and then negotiate their deals."

"They?"

Maya didn't answer right away.

"The *clients*," she eventually said. "Big-time powerful dudes."

Leonard scowled. "I can't even picture it. Sounds like a horse auction."

"It got to the point this year where I only had one client anyway. He wanted me all to himself."

"This Lucio fella?"

"No, no. It's the guy who liked to tell me things. Don't know if I should say who. He's famous."

"The same one wanted you dumped like garbage?"

Maya didn't answer but a trembling lip betrayed her. She spent a full minute wiping away the tears.

"I shouldn't have said anything," she said. "It's not over. They'll come after me. I know about things they don't want the world knowing. They find out you killed Jason, they'll do the same to you."

Leonard only shook his head with a defiant look in his eyes.

"I'd like to see them sons of bitches try it."

They were quiet for a while. Maya bowed her head, clutched her stomach as she cramped. Leonard rose and took the pie from the oven, put a kettle on, and then fixed her a tall cup of soda, grapefruit juice, whiskey, and hot water. He handed the drink to her and winked.

"This'll cure the guilt off a preacher."

"What is it?"

"Hillbilly aspirin."

She braced the mug with two hands and took a sip. Made a childish face of disgust.

"Damn," she said.

"Drink up and let's eat."

Maya ate heartily, and when she had finished her meal, she said, "Part of me feels guilty for just being alive."

"What do you mean?"

"It's what he does to you," she said. "Makes you think you can't take a breath without his permission. And the other guy—the client—he just smothers you. Thing is they are both mixed up with drugs now. Something big. Mixed up with some really dangerous people."

Leonard waited a moment, as if trying to choose his words carefully. Then he reached over and squeezed her shoulder gently.

"What I know is, I thought that the world owed me a living, and I worked hard to collect on it," he said. "But those men after you? They used young girls for their gain, like it was owed to them. A tribute to the devil in them. If these men show up on my land, Maya, and want to get hard about it, well, let 'em come. They'll live just long enough to regret it."

Maya felt a chill, captivated by the suddenly distant and deranged look about Leonard. They stared out the rain-streaked window for a time and listened to the patter. A needy cat wandered past her shin, looking for a stroking. Then Maya nudged the mason jar of whiskey toward Leonard and smiled.

Maya helped him clean the table and do the dishes. It was past ten when the rain moved on and a waning moon rose in the sky. The night air became charged with the sound of katydids and whip-poor-wills. Resting on a nearby shelf was a pair of matching antlers, twelve pointers with an unusual drop tine on one side. Maya fingered the tine, clearly fascinated. Leonard watched her, and then explained how bucks were still in velvet in late summer, their antlers covered in a skin that fed the bone and helped it grow faster.

"I'd never seen a deer before until I got here," she said.

To Leonard it was like saying she had never seen a tree or a cloud until now.

"Stick around here, and you'll see plenty. Watch the pear tree in the yard. About this time whitetails cross the field to eat them all up."

"Is that bad?"

Leonard shook his head and smiled.

"Not necessarily. That's how you get yourself more pear trees."

"Huh?"

"I'll explain another day," he said. "Besides, every now and then I'll pick one off with my thirty aught for jerky and consider the trade fair."

While Leonard turned off lights, Maya retreated to the bedroom with the bag of clothes and toiletries. She brushed her hair again and then lay down on the bed and yawned.

A few minutes later Leonard knocked. She sat up sleepily.

"Come in, Leonard."

He poked his head in.

"Before you drift off, something I wanted to show you."

He gestured for her to follow him, and they walked down the stairs and stopped near the front door.

"See that rug there," he said.

"Yeah?"

"Pull it up."

She reached down and pulled up one edge of the wool rug. It snagged. Several strands of piano wire snapped taut. Maya yanked harder and with a creak a hinged section of the wide plank flooring lifted, revealing a crawl space beneath the rug.

She gave him a look.

"Place to hide," he said. "Just don't let anyone see you."

"Where's it go?"

Leonard pointed toward the front door.

"Tunnel that way takes you to the barn."

"And that way?" she said, looking the other direction.

"East toward the woods, where you'll find the entrance to a cave. Don't want to go that way unless you got a hundred years to find your way out."

Maya let the hatch close.

"See how the rug covers it right up?" he said.

"How many more secrets you got, Leonard?"

He favored her with a sly grin. Maya noticed the shotgun propped in a corner. She wondered how many more guns he had around the place and what else he might have hidden on his land.

"Secrets the only thing keeps this world together," he said and showed Maya back to her room.

That night Maya dreamed of a long dinner table, with Lucio and The Mayor seated at one end and she and Leonard at the other. Faceless phantoms served a meal, thrusting plates in front of them for inspection. On the platters were heaps of bone and rancid meat piled high. The men dug in, tearing, gnawing, their appetites as grotesque as their enthusiasm. Maya only watched, refusing when Leonard offered her a rabbit leg, thinking in the dream that he had betrayed her. She knew she had to run, to get away, but her muscles were knotted, her body paralyzed.

And then she looked down and saw her feet were bolted to the floor.

When she screamed, Lucio and The Mayor looked up from their meal and, their mouths full of gore, they smiled.

The Mayor rose and started toward her.

She must have been screaming in her sleep. She heard Leonard's voice now, soothing words half-sung like a lullaby, the man's voice frail and unsure of itself. A hand patted the scar tissue on her back. Maya muttered incoherently. Abruptly she mumbled words of gratitude and turned on her side.

Maya heard his voice again, distant, unclear, but the night terror had passed thanks to his calming presence.

SEVEN

It was Grimes's idea to take the cargo van.

The Econoline belonged to ReBirth Baptist Missionary, a mega-church on the city's south side whose pastor, a client of Lucio's, had a penchant for pigtails. The van was inconspicuous, in good condition, had working taillights and would provide cover for two large men and a bag of firearms.

It had also been Grimes's idea that they wear their Sunday best.

They left around noontime, driving across Georgia's Piedmont region, hitting rain as showers freight-trained west to east across the state. The land was characterized by unremarkable interstate exits, pastures, and forests of loblolly pine. Grimes took U.S. 27 south through Columbus, and by the time they arrived in Trickum County, the skies had cleared and an hour of daylight remained.

Grimes drove up and down the lake roads, looking for landmarks. Nothing but wilderness, wiregrass, pitch pines, other hardwoods marked with blue slashes designating property boundaries, elsewhere orange and yellow slashes at stump level that identified trees to be culled.

The map had a topographic legend. Lot numbers. William sat in the passenger seat, attempting to translate.

"I remember a crooked shack," he said, looking up from the map.

"Was down here scouting with Lucio a few months back. I remember where that is. It's an old voting booth," Grimes said.

They passed a roadside vegetable stand advertising boiled peanuts. A few farmers stood beside carts of produce, talking among themselves, fanning at the gnats that swarmed around their heads.

"Question is," William said, "why would Lucio buy so much land way the hell down here?"

Grimes smiled. "You can't bury all that cash in the ground. But you can bury tractor trailers. Lucio, see, he's got a plan."

"What kind of plan?"

Grimes cocked an eye at William, who still scratched at the wounds healing across his chest and back.

"Underground grow labs and privacy. That's what land can get you. You dig?"

William nodded.

"So how did some old swamper get the drop on you anyhow? He dragged you pretty good, huh?"

William stared out the window, a look of shame coming into his face.

"Won't compare to how I'm going to do him," he said.

The sun had the tint of an eye infection. They drove deep into the county, passing cotton fields, the light withdrawing behind rows of planted pines that served as a natural boundary between tracts. The fields gave way to weedy yards and trailers with big satellite dishes. Barns. Farmhouses. Small plots of gravestones all bearing the same family name.

At dusk Grimes slowed and turned into the lot of a concrete block building. There was a water-stained turquoise awning, signs for Schlitz and Mello Yello, a bucket of sand by the door full of cigarette butts. A few cars were parked in the gravel lot of the juke joint. A telephone pole leaned precariously over the building as if waiting for one more burst of wind to bring it down.

"What's this?" William said.

"Easy, man. We're meeting a friend of Lucio's."

Before William could ask more questions, Grimes was out of the van and walking toward the front door.

William slammed the passenger-side door, noticed his cousin Kevin's car was already there.

He did not, however, notice the Crown Vic with government plates.

Kevin was playing a pinball game when William and a man he didn't know stepped into the Owl's Roost. A few heads turned, including the cop at the bar, his moon-shaped face anchored by a bushy mustache, hair washing away in the shower strand by strand. Kevin glimpsed the badge attached to the man's belt swallowed up by belly fat.

Ronnie Prance, beer in hand, followed William and Grimes to a corner table out of earshot.

William spotted Kevin and waved him over.

The Owl's Roost had an eight-by-six-foot parquet dance floor. A musician sat on a stool, small amplifier at his feet, plucking the bass string of a Telecaster while the cigarette in his mouth burned down to the filter. At first his drone sounded amateurish, as if the man hadn't held a guitar before that afternoon and was learning as he played. But a languorous rhythm emerged. The old bluesman didn't sing so much as hum, but there was anguish in the sounds he made.

William popped Grimes on the shoulder and pointed at Kevin.

"This is my cousin," he said.

Grimes nodded. William eyed the local cop, yet to be introduced, who was busy examining something afloat in his beer.

"Who is this?"

Ronnie Prance looked up.

"Nobody," he said.

"Meet *nobody*," Grimes said.

"So what do you know?" William said.

Kevin supplied a piece of receipt paper from the pharmacy where Ronelle worked.

"What the hell is that?" Prance said.

"Guy went to the doctor once for a heart problem, *nitro*-something." Kevin said. "Got his address and maps of the road that takes you to his property."

Prance glared at Grimes.

"I could have told you where that batshit bootlegger lived—miles into the backcountry. It's a maze of old logging roads and firebreaks out that way."

"Well, that's good to know now," William said. "My cousin came through anyway."

Prance shrugged. "So give him a participation trophy."

Grimes looked at Prance. "You tracking?"

"Sure," Prance said. "I know you figure me for a pig with more vises than a hardware store. But I got the message loud and clear. Help with the land grabs. Ignore the traffic through the county, and when I do pinch a runner make the investigation sloppy. Sound like I'm tracking?"

"Indeed."

"If there's one thing I'm good at," Prance said. "It's botching police work and passing blame."

"For a girl a month and nice little envelope, right?"

"I like them Puerto Rican ones with big behinds. Got five grand on the Georgia game this Saturday, too. It's a wonderful life, so don't begrudge me my amusements. But I do want to know a few things."

"Such as?"

"Why am I here? And why are you messing with an old kook like Leonard Moye?"

Grimes leaned across the table.

"Little extra security. You on the clock?"

"I make my own hours."

"What do you know about this Leonard guy?"

Prance elaborately stubbed out his cigarette, giving him thinking time.

"My daddy bought liquor from him. Hell, everybody did. He's lived out in them backwoods his whole life. You know, there was a time when bootlegging was considered an honorable profession. Revenuers used to poke the fields with sharp sticks looking for Leonard's stock. They'd chase him down dirt roads, hide in bushes, and try to wait him out. But Leonard was what you might call a savant when it came to revenue agents. He'd switch cars. Booby-trap bridges. Might've hid his liquor in barrels of turpentine. Never proven but rumor is Leonard burned down the tax assessor's office in '73, making him a hero to the old-timers 'round here. After Leonard's wife disappeared he had some sort of breakdown. Every now and then you'll see him driving around town with a mannequin dressed in his wife's clothes. Totally out to lunch. Remind me again why it is you give a shit about him?"

"He's got one of Lucio's bitches hiding in his house," William said to his instant regret. "She might've talked to that narc got capped."

Grimes shot him a look that would coldcock a mule, glancing at Kevin next. *Get amnesia, boy*, his eyes said.

To Prance, Grimes offered a revision.

"See, this is how it is, we believe Leonard has some property that belongs to the outfit I work for. After much consideration, management has decided they would like to have that property back."

Prance nodded, amused.

"You're a smooth one. Used to be a cop, too, didn't you?"

"How many heart attacks you had since you sat down?" Grimes said.

Prance drained his beer and wiped his whiskers.

"So aside from keeping things secure, what's the rest of my involvement?"

"You'll be the one to find Leonard deceased. Natural causes."

Prance considered the implications.

"Well, now. With no will or next of kin the property would go to probate court, wouldn't it? I'm certain there is a sympathetic magistrate hereabout that would consider an offer made by a qualified investor to be fair, as would be his dutiful intention to preserve the integrity of Leonard's land."

Grimes smiled.

"Something like that, yeah."

"This shit just fell in your lap, didn't it?" Prance said.

"Consider it a happy accident. We still want our, let's say, personal property back."

"And you're sure Leonard has this—*property*?"

Grimes nodded.

"And what if he doesn't?"

The bluesman was croaking a sorrowful tune. The first wave of backdoor juke-jointers had arrived. Two by two, the dance floor was slowly filling. One shapely woman balanced on the ball of her right foot and shook her left leg as if ants were crawling up the thigh. The four men paused to appreciate her improvisation.

"Looks to be a beautiful evening for natural causes," Grimes said as Prance got up to leave.

After a lazy day about the house Maya took an afternoon nap. Leonard was about to wake her when he heard her stirring in the bathroom.

Twenty minutes later Maya appeared looking well rested, wearing one of the tank tops he had bought her, ill-fitting jeans cuffed to the shins and cinched with a belt that seemed familiar to Leonard.

"I found it," she said off his look. "You don't mind, do you?"

"Forgot about that old mule chest in the bedroom," he said. "No telling what you'll find in there. Never was one to throw anything away. Coffee?"

"Extra sugar."

There was a flattop blanket chest in front of the settee. It was made of yellow pine, the wood darkened with age. On a nearby huntboard were empty picture frames, an ashtray, feminine knick-knacks and a leather-bound copy of the King James Bible, which Maya opened curiously, pages to her touch soft as down feathers. She read a passage and then closed her eyes and lifted her chin as though summoning some power inside her.

"*Wherefore, my beloved brethren, let every man be swift to hear, slow to speak, slow to wrath—*"

"*For the wrath of man worketh not the righteousness of God,*" Leonard said. He handed her a cup of coffee. "Book of James. You know the Bible?"

"First time reading it. Got a knack for memorizing things."

"That's quite a talent. I can't even remember what I had for breakfast."

"Unfortunately it's what got me in this fix."

"How so?"

Maya picked up a picture frame, noticing fingerprints on the dusty glass.

"You know about all the land being sold down here? Thousands of acres?"

"Might've heard something about it."

"Well, I know all there is to know. Shell companies buying the land, loans from foreign banks, offshore accounts, shady bankers, prosecutors, judges, and cops bought and paid for and a big drug cartel behind it all."

Leonard raised an eyebrow and sipped his coffee.

"How you know all that? Your client—the famous one?"

Maya nodded.

"Why would he do that?"

"Big ego," she said. "He likes to brag. Doesn't think anything will ever happen to him."

Maya shrugged. She glanced at the mannequin in the rocking chair, Marjean positioned so as to face the windows. Outside she saw dirt daubers tucked into a corner of the porch's slant roof, their nest of tubes resembling a pan flute long bereft of any music. Nearby a leather boot hung on a hook. Birds had nested inside it. Maya's thoughts drifted and momentarily she thought she saw the chair begin to rock just as Leonard's voice snapped her out of her reverie.

"Sounds like a damn fool."

Maya shrugged.

"Some people get away with dirty deeds their whole life. How the world works."

Maya held the mug in two hands and savored another sip. Most of the girls she had known hadn't cared for coffee. And sweets had been denied them—Lucio's rules. Coffee-stained teeth and sugar rotted them. A memory of one of his men going room to room handing out condoms along with whitening toothpaste made her shudder, so much the coffee almost spilled.

"You know I dreamed about you last night," she said with a blush.

"Hope it wasn't me made you scream that away."

"I screamed?"

"Nightmare had the cats with their backs up."

"You sang to me, didn't you?"

She smiled at him. Leonard nodded a little sheepishly.

"Don't tell anybody," he said. "I got a reputation to think about."

She took another sip of coffee and licked her lips. Her eyes were drawn to the empty picture frames. She gestured to the huntboard.

"Why don't you have any photos?"

Leonard shrugged. "Used to. Suppose I got tired of looking at them."

"How long since Marjean died?"

Leonard walked over and put his hand on the mannequin's shoulder. There was a black cat asleep in Marjean's lap. The cat yawned, then reached out and flexed a front paw before closing its eyes again. Leonard struggled to meet Maya's inquisitive eyes.

"You see them cedar waxwings there?" he said, pointing outside.

Maya took a step toward him and looked out the windows.

"They're pretty."

"Seem to be leaving later and later every year," he said.

Maya toed the plank floor, wondering how he would react if she said what was on her mind.

"I was thinking that maybe I ought to go to the police after all."

Leonard's eyes were on the large steel casement window. He worried a tooth with his tongue as if deep in thought.

"How about we take some air? Help me check my lines."

"Check your what?"

He smiled coyly, and then motioned for Maya to follow him outside.

Leonard offered her a peppermint stick and they lit out for the creek, the Marlin leveraction slung over one shoulder, and his revolver in a leather holster. Maya followed, feeling oddly secure in spite of her predicament.

A few hundred yards from the homestead they arrived at the edge of a transition zone, planted pines giving way to an old growth forest full of towering oak trees. Behind them the scarecrows were like artifacts for visitors from a distant future to puzzle over. The gnats were a nuisance. Maya swore at those blackening the licked end of her peppermint stick.

"Motherfuckers," she said irritably.

Leonard looked back, not breaking stride.

"They'll thin out," he assured her. "Gnats are considered a condiment in these parts."

Maya fanned the air around her head.

"They don't seem to bother *you* much."

"Reckon you taste better than I do."

They skirted dense honeysuckle growing unchecked along the ground and then came to a clearing, the sight of a controlled burn from the previous year, which Leonard pointed out to Maya. Fresh vegetation had sprouted over the summer. They continued on deeper into the woods. He showed her the sites where he had once buried barrels of turpentine with liquor secreted inside, what looked like tortoise holes or the narrow mouth of a cave. He explained to Maya how he used an old-fashioned kerosene pump to draw the whiskey out, the leaves of the big white oaks perfect cover from the probing sticks of revenuers.

Leonard walked slowly, mindful of snakes. At his request Maya didn't wander and shadowed his footsteps. The trees thinned along the ridge and they hiked down into a draw. They followed the water, a brook eventually leading to a small pond covered in lily pads. A sun-bleached tree trunk rose from the center of the water like a crooked finger. The air was sultry. A dragonfly hovered briefly before Maya's face. She made a noise.

"Tell me that thing doesn't bite?"

He shook his head and smiled.

"Only flies and skeeters."

But Maya wasn't soothed. She was a city girl, not country, and bewildered to find herself in the thick of raw nature, eyes darting at every winged insect, their buzzing enough to make her skin prickle as she scratched phantom itches on her neck and arms, or slapped at the touch of a wayward spider webbing.

"Couldn't do it," she said. "No makeup, no heels. No room service."

"Takes some getting' used to, Maya. But I bet you could. I know you could."

They arrived at the edge of a slough. He wiped his brow with a handkerchief. Paused to catch his breath. Then he pointed out to Maya the rope running the width of the creek, the shirttail nets barely visible beneath the water's surface.

"The nets are like a fence," he said by way of explanation. "They filter the water there. Fish try and force a way through and get caught by the gills."

Maya lit a menthol and smoked awkwardly, the cigarette pinched between two knuckles. But the nicotine had a calming effect, and the smoke seemed to keep the bugs away. She eyed the stagnant water, the ripples created by a swarm of whirligig beetles.

"What kind of fish do you catch?"

"You name it," he said. "But my favorite kind is partial to this spot."

She made a face, watching as he leaned the lever-action rifle against an abutment and removed the holster and pistol from his belt. After a quick look around, he waded into the water, hoisting the nets one at a time for inspection. Five minutes later, he returned with a net full of mostly asphyxiated redhorse suckers, his field pants soaked to the waist and globs of mud on the toes of his brogans.

"Here," he said and held out the net.

She grabbed the cinched end, alarmed as one fish began to writhe.

"What's wrong with that one?"

"Must've just been caught."

She held the net up as if appraising the weight.

"How do they breathe water?"

"Fish got to keep moving. They open their mouths and let water into the gills. The gills get oxygen from the water."

She watched the fish's mouth open and close, a flat, dead expression on its face. For an instant she saw herself in that net, floundering with all the other girls, a hand holding them to a crowd at auction.

"I thought they just held their breath for a long-ass time."

Leonard laughed.

"You haven't had much schooling, have you?"

She handed him the net and looked upstream, her expression souring. Spanish moss stirred along the limbs of a live oak. Kingbirds squawked above them.

Noting her silence, Leonard said, "Wasn't trying to imply you're ignorant."

"Well, I'm not," Maya said. But anger flashed in her eyes.

"Just wanted to say nether did I. Learned all I know out here," Leonard said, pointing across the stream. "Know how much schooling you might've had?"

Maya dropped her cigarette in the inch of silt on which she stood.

"I don't know. One day I was going to school," she said. "Next day I wasn't. Happened so fast I never thought about it since. Learned mostly by listening to clients. Lawyers, bankers—politicians."

Leonard adjusted his glasses and regarded her for a moment.

"Been thinking about what all that you've seen around here."

Their attention was drawn to the net. The fish had stopped spasming.

"Like a dead body you mean?"

"Like a dead body."

It took a minute before she found the right words, recalling language used by none other than Lucio himself.

"Way I see it," she said. "Police and Jason don't deserve each other's company."

They favored each other with smiles and with that the two conspirators walked back up the ridge and into the hardwoods, Maya finding comfort in another cigarette, Leonard finding his in the promise of his troubled guest perhaps escaping her past for good.

Maya declined the offer to help him scale the suckers, the smell and chunky insides making her queasy. Leonard dumped the guts in a bucket while the oil in a skillet atop the stove heated up. He breaded the fillets and set them aside, humming a tune, hunched over a cutting board as flies dive-bombed the fish innards.

Sun-fatigued and a bit drowsy, she sipped sweet tea at the kitchen table instead. The number of insects diminished. The cats were attentive, playful, swatting and pawing at the flies until the flies stopped moving.

The black cat she had seen in Marjean's lap hopped into her own and began bathing. A female, on the small side, lean, eyes yellow as egg yolk, with pointy white teeth. Maya rubbed the cat's nose. Smiled when the cat licked her finger.

"Now that's a sight."

Maya looked up. Leonard was rubbing his hands with a dishrag.

"This one likes me."

"That old girl never liked nobody but Marjean."

"Marjean won't be jealous, will she?" Maya said.

Her humor was lost on him though. Leonard looked into the living room, at the mannequin by the window.

"You're not jealous of Maya now, is you, sweetheart?"

Maya smiled. The cat in her lap began to purr.

"Well, is she?"

"Marjean says you can have her. About time she found a new lap to sleep on."

Maya ran a knuckle against the cat's whiskers, first the left side of its mouth, then the right. The cat angled her head slightly, indicating she'd like some loving along the jaw and neck.

"Can I name her?"

"Reckon yes, since you got Marjean's blessing."

After some contemplation, Maya said, "Think I'll name her *Miss Annie*."

"Miss Annie? How'd you drum up that name?"

"Saw it in that book there," Maya said, pointing to the Sears Roebuck catalog on the sugar chest behind him.

"This old thing?" Leonard said.

He picked up the catalog, fingering the smudged cover. He flipped past pictures of ladies' housedresses, union suits, Honor

Bilt homes, and Ranger repeating target rifles. He told Maya how excited his mother would get every time the new catalog arrived. He eventually stopped at a dog-eared advertisement for *Little Orphan Annie's Treasure Hunt*.

"It's a pretty name—*Annie*," he said, a catch in his voice, yet when he looked over at Maya he knew she had been too preoccupied with the cat to have heard it.

The suckers cooked quickly in the deep fat, and by nightfall the kitchen was rich with the odor of fried fish and potatoes. The fillets curlicued in the hot oil. What bones were left dissolved completely. Leonard hustled to the living room and returned with Marjean, her wig askew, a stiff arm sticking straight out. After seating the mannequin, he served Maya. She pinched a bit of fish between her fingers and offered it to her new companion.

"You stop that before all the others get jealous," Leonard said.

"Annie likes it. I like it, too."

Maya drank two refills of sweet tea and added extra salt and pepper on her potatoes. The cats were talkative and needy. Leonard cut his last fillet into equal portions and gave them to the cats gathered around his chair.

Maya didn't notice when he rose suddenly from the table and, back to the wall, dimmed a hurricane lamp by the sink, cupped his hands around his eyes, and peered through the window. In the distance a beam of light ghosted over barn doors.

"Remember that hiding place, Maya?" he said urgently. "Get you there now."

It wasn't Leonard's words but his tone that got her moving fast.

"What is it?"

Leonard already had the lever-action rifle in his hand.

"Don't come out unless you hear me tell you. Could be some shooting."

"Oh my God, Leonard—?"

"Won't be me getting shot. Hush now."

She went cold from fear. Leonard followed her toward the front door, turning off lights as they went. He yanked back the throw rug and lifted the hatch in the floor.

"Go on. Now."

He patted her gently. Held one hand as Maya lowered herself into the dark maw of the crawl space. She had to lie flat so Leonard could close the hatch, and gasped when she heard the click of the latch lock. A dank smell pervaded the tunnel.

Maya covered her mouth. Tears trickled across her knuckles. The sound of Leonard's footsteps faded. She heard chair legs scraping across the floor.

A door closed.

Another opened.

Then all was silent in the house.

Gregory Grimes, William, and his cousin Kevin made several turns, following Prance's unmarked Crown Vic alongside an irrigation ditch. In the dusky light they glimpsed a field of cotton off to the east. Thick vegetation grew on the other side of the firebreak and the limbs of ancient oak trees formed a natural canopy above the hardpan roads. Ahead in the middle of the break a bachelor group of bucks froze, alert to the two-car convoy, before the deer bounded away. William looked back at his cousin.

"You up for this?"

Kevin nodded, but both hands were trembling in the pocket of his hooded sweatshirt.

"No names," William said by way of reminder. "Don't even talk. Just extra eyes and ears is all I'm asking for. Be a little something for you when we get done."

Brake lights winked ahead of them. Ronnie Prance rolled down the driver's window and pointed to the trailhead. Grimes pulled the van up beside Prance's car.

"Straight through those woods and you'll hit a big drainage. Follow that draw south, and Leonard's place is maybe four, five hundred yards yonder."

"Where are you going to be?" Grimes said.

"Oh, I'll be around. Waiting on them natural causes," Prance said, and put his window up.

Grimes backed up and parked facing the firebreak. Without a word to William or Kevin he got out and walked around to the rear of the van.

He opened the doors and removed a duffel bag from beneath the bench seat. In the bag were a .40 caliber semiautomatic Smith & Wesson and a .357 caliber J-frame revolver, along with a paddle holster for the full-sized semi and a right-handed leather ankle holster for the snubbie. Grimes gunned up, feeling their eyes on him.

Zip-tie handcuffs. Duct tape. Binoculars and a four-cell flashlight.

"What about my piece?" William said.

Grimes searched the bag, handed him a .40 caliber Glock 27 with a plugged barrel and a magazine that unbeknownst to William was filled with blank cartridges.

"That's it?"

"That's it, partner. For you."

"I told you this fool had shotguns and rifles. Want me backing you with *this*?" William said, holding up the subcompact to make his point.

Grimes turned his back on William and Kevin to pull another weapon from the duffel, a carbine Uzi equipped with an underfolding stock. He had done the conversion to full auto himself, bringing along three thirty-two-round magazines. Grimes waved the carbine at them and grinned.

"Don't you worry about firepower," he said.

The humidity had them all running with sweat.

By dark they reached the draw and followed it through hardwood bottoms. After a quarter of a mile they climbed a ridge and hit the barbwire fence.

"This is it," William said. "I remember now."

Grimes killed the light. They followed a cow path that ran adjacent to the fence. There was an overgrown field of wheat and goldenrod to the west. After a time the field began to stretch and roll gently down toward Leonard's homestead.

"Look," William said, pointing ahead. "There are them scarecrows I told you about."

"Don't seem like nobody's home," Kevin said.

Grimes grabbed his binoculars, satisfied there was enough moonlight to glass the property. The house and barn sat in a U-shaped bowl, thick timber surrounding it on all sides. Nearest them, a large barn loomed ahead, and a windmill. The glow of a lamp behind a curtained first-floor window gave Grimes an idea of the size of the house. Stars salted the sky, the low-riding moon illuminated the scarecrows in the field.

Kevin, feeling a little spooked, said, "What's up with those things? He doesn't grow anything out here. Why does he have so many scarecrows for?"

"Maybe one of them isn't a scarecrow?" William said.

Kevin squinted at the occupied field of straw men, some arranged on X-shaped posts like victims of a mass crucifixion.

Grimes handed the binoculars to Kevin.

"You know how to whistle?"

"Yeah."

"You see anything moving, let one rip."

"What's the plan?" William said.

He pulled a small tactical flashlight from his belt and handed it to William.

"Check the barn," Grimes told him. "I'll cover the house."

Grimes was already moving away from them and disappeared into the pines on the eastern edge of the tract.

William took a few tentative steps into the field, the Glock in one hand, Maglite in the other. Far enough away from the house, he turned on the flashlight and played the beam around, spotting one scarecrow, then another, the sudden reality of each, and an illusion of movement causing his balls to shrink. Breathing heavy, he jerked around with the gun leveled when he heard his cousin disobey Grimes's order by following him.

Without a word, William shone his light over the double doors of the old barn. It had a gable roof, twice as long as wide with hinged cladding boards on the north face opened for ventilation. Corded tractor tires were stacked against a wall. William glanced back in annoyance at Kevin. Then he slowly opened one of the barn doors, wincing at the noise of creaking wood and rusted hinges. He kept a low profile behind the door as it swung open.

William and Kevin looked inside. Tier poles and crossbeams extended the length of the barn. On the floor, the seven-passenger Studebaker, the Hudson, and a Chevy C10 long bed were parked bumper to bumper. There was a heavy odor in the air, like kerosene and aged wood. William cast the light in a slow, sweeping arc until satisfied the barn was vacant. He noted the pot still and a row of white oak barrels.

"What is that?" Kevin said.

William approached the copper still.

"White Lightnin'."

"Maybe we should go on to the house?"

But William placed a hand on the nearest barrel, feeling the smooth, sanded surface of the staves. The barrels appeared empty, the still not in use. Mason jars on a shelf were covered with dust.

"I wonder how much this is worth?"

"I think somebody's in here with us," Kevin said.

William whirled, pointing the .40 at a glowing hurricane lamp at the far end of the center breezeway. Hung by its handle from a nail.

They hadn't heard a sound.

Kevin moved sideways toward a workbench, thinking to grab something heavy for a weapon. He picked up a locking wrench. A door rattled shut. Wood creaked as if a ladder were being climbed. Kevin froze. William played the light across the breezeway, then up to the loft. He kept the Glock level, crossing the flashlight beneath his shooting hand in the manner of cops he had seen on television shows.

He slowly approached the end of the threshing floor, pausing to check the interior of the Studebaker. Sweat burned his eyes. He steadied the flashlight beam, the nimbus of the hurricane lamp illuminating a storage room and the plank door that might've been closed moments ago.

Instinct told William the old man was in there.

He turned the flashlight off and crouched against the wall adjacent to the door. He motioned for his cousin to stay back. Then he switched the Glock to his left hand and, after some deliberation, reached for the door handle and yanked, staying low as he pulled it toward him. William felt the door drag, followed instantly by a deafening *one-two* blast. William covered his head as the door and wall opposite him was peppered with buckshot.

William and Kevin took off. A rifle firing stopped them in their tracks.

"Behind you, boys."

When William and his cousin turned around they were face-to-face with Leonard Moye.

"Some time ago poachers got to sneaking on my land. Stole whiskey from that room before I could move it. Thought they could walk right in and help themselves," Leonard said. "That double-barrel booby trap solved my problem."

Leonard held the 30-30 at his hip, trained on William. Kevin dropped the wrench and began to back away. But William did an unwise thing. He jerked the pistol up and pulled the trigger.

It was panic fire. William emptied the ten rounds in seconds. Leonard looked down at his chest, surprised to still be standing, let alone unharmed. Then he raised the 30-30 to his shoulder, aiming between the two men. William stared at the semiauto in his hand.

"Blanks? Gregory, you dirty mother—fu—"

"He's not human," Kevin said, throwing up his hands. "He's the devil."

"Something wrong with your popgun?"

"Hold on a minute now," William said and looked at Leonard. He dropped the Glock. Gestured in a peaceable way. "We're just here for the girl. *Just* the girl."

"You believe in miracles?" Leonard said.

"No—wait—I—?"

"Me neither," Leonard said.

He shot William dead center of his forehead.

Some of the mess coming out the back of his head hit Kevin in the face. Kevin flinched, mouth ajar, his eyes wide and unbelieving. Leonard winked at him and worked the lever of the 30-30.

Kevin spun to his left, almost knocking himself unconscious against a post as he fled the barn.

Leonard stepped over William's splayed body, watching in amusement as Kevin sprinted across the field, a shadow by starlight disappearing among the scarecrows and hay bales.

Maya suppressed a cough with her hands. She heard noises in the house and prayed it was Leonard coming back. But the footsteps were too measured, too cautious. The floor creaked above her. She didn't dare move.

That's when a cat began to yowl.

Grimes stood a few feet from the front door when he heard the rifle shot and a commotion in the barn. He waited, his lip curling grimly at the sound of the .40 firing blanks. He looked through a nearby window. The house was dark.

He tried the door and was surprised to find it unlocked.

Moonlight shone in the small foyer. There was a woven throw rug on the floor. Kitchen was off to the left, a hallway ahead. A short flight of stairs led to a second floor. But Grimes fixed his attention on the living room and the silhouette of a person, what looked like a woman seated in a rocking chair.

The floor groaned under his weight. He watched the woman, anticipating a startled movement, maybe a scream. But she didn't budge.

Then the chair began to rock.

Grimes's finger wrapped around the trigger of the Uzi when he saw the shape of a cat jump from the rocker and fly past him, stopping to claw at the rug in the foyer. Grimes moved closer to see the woman better. He noticed the lopsided wig first, a profile pale as an ice sheet and those vacant eyes.

He shook his head and backed out of the living room. The cat was crying louder now, claws digging at the woven rug. Grimes listened, and then kicked the cat off the rug.

He heard a muffled sound of distress. Then Grimes bent over and threw the rug aside.

"Jackpot," he said and tried to lift the hidden door. It was locked.

Maya rolled onto her stomach and was squirming away when a single pistol shot exploded. She screamed and banged her head on the roof of the tunnel.

As soon as Grimes realized the trapdoor was locked, he drew his pistol and fired a round at the old padlock, splitting it in two. He kicked the lock away, holstered the semiautomatic. When he lifted the hatch he saw Maya's skinny legs as if she were trying to swim deeper into the tunnel. He reached down with one hand, caught her by a foot, and pulled her out.

"Oh, I got you now," he said.

Grimes dragged her through the door to the front yard.

On her back, kicking and screaming, she saw Grimes backlit by the moon, looming over her with a sinister glint in his eyes. Until she saw a figure moving swiftly up behind him.

Grimes started to turn, too late.

Leonard cinched the feed sack around Grimes's neck. Grimes listed to the left, struggling with the rope. He made choking sounds. Maya smelled gasoline.

She crawled on hands and knees away from Grimes. With one hand working at the sack covering his head, the other found the grip of the Uzi. Grimes squeezed the trigger and arced a salvo into the sky. Coyotes answered him, calling from somewhere deep in the pine flats. Maya was halfway to the front door when she heard Leonard's voice.

"You might not want to see this, Maya," he said.

Grimes fell to one knee. His chest heaved drastically.

"Get up, you sorry rat," Leonard said with a tug of the rope.

Grimes jerked right and fired, stitching a nearby cedar tree. Instinct told him to exhaust the clip in a 360-degree motion. Guaranteed to hit someone if he did. He could feel the rope grow taut, however, knew the man was wrangling him like a steer. Gasping for air, Grimes tripped in a flower bed. Fired again, hitting the ground. Maya covered her ears and screamed. If Grimes had aimed the Uzi at his three o'clock Maya would have been dead.

But the rope went slack.

A moment later Maya saw Leonard strike a match against his wristwatch and cupped his hands.

Then he lit the gunman's head on fire.

Grimes started at the sound of the match head igniting. It took a couple of seconds for him to feel the heat, for his hair to start crisping, the aged cloth burning like flash paper and blistering his skin. Wild with terror, he ran, only wanting the burning to stop. The Uzi fell from his shoulder to the ground. Grimes yanked up his hooded sweatshirt, trying to smother the flames.

His lungs filled with fire.

Kevin had stopped to catch his breath among clumps of dog fennel in the heart of the field. The scarecrows were positioned all around him, a Grand Guignol of crooked grins and button eyes, standing witness to a well-preserved little clearing. There were two grave-stones, the plots unequal, one adult-sized, and the other probably for a small child. Kevin took a knee, trying to read the stones by moonlight.

Marjean Mo-- ...beloved... die-

The second, smaller marker was nearly illegible. The only words Kevin could discern.

Annabelle...

He tensed at the sounds of Grimes's muffled screaming. He got up, ran through the tall grass until he could see Leonard's house and barn were a hundred yards away.

As if Kevin needed any more evidence this was a field of hor-rors, he saw Grimes stumbling, running erratically, enormous head ablaze.

Grimes began to slow, but his momentum kept him going for thirty more yards toward Kevin, until, in a sparky cloud of burnt cloth and flesh, he collapsed. His arms and legs flailed briefly. Then he was still, smoking flickers of flame head to toe.

Kevin turned north and sprinted toward the wood line, a vision of Leonard Moye in his head, Leonard as a bulletproof Lucifer, claiming souls in his ghostly fields.

He ran, thinking he was as good as dead himself.

Ronnie Prance let down a window and smoked a cigarette, just waiting in the croaking dark. The pinewoods filled with nocturnal chatter. He heard the shrill cry of a fox rise, the snaps and clacks of treehoppers, the collective twang of frogs.

As a boy Prance had seen a panther in those woods, a rare daytime sighting, its paws as big as catcher's mitts. The panther had turned its head and acknowledged him briefly, almost dismissively, before continuing on.

Prance heard the sound of Grimes's Uzi submachine gun way off in the distance.

It sounded like panic fire and went unanswered.

Prance reached for the pistol holstered under his belly fat.

The shooting stopped. After a few minutes he was all but ready to kick the Crown Vic in reverse and get the hell out of there. But what would Lucio say to that? He shook his head and belched from indigestion.

"I'm not going out there," he said aloud.

No goddamn way.

By the time he got the beam of a door-mounted spotlight on the woods beyond the trailhead Kevin had appeared, scared and winded. He yanked open the passenger door and jumped in.

"Go! Just go! God, man, please, get us out of here!"

Prance pointed the gun at Kevin, who didn't seem to notice. He was hyperventilating.

"What the hell happened?"

"He burned up Grimes. Luvagod, go!"

"What?" Prance said. "What about William?"

"Dead," Kevin said between gasps. "Shot him through the head. That's no man back there. He's the devil!"

Kevin's clothes were torn. There was blood on his face, mostly William's. Prance put the car in reverse, his eyes on the woods, and then drove back up the firebreak.

"What about the girl?" he said. "She still alive?"

Kevin couldn't answer. He was doubled over in the seat, rocking like a child, the only words he could muster a warning about the devil in their midst.

On the south side of town, Prance dropped Kevin off a couple of blocks from his house. By then, the fear bled out of him, Kevin was nearly catatonic. Prance aimed a finger at him.

"Clean yourself up. Not a word of this, you hear me?"

Kevin nodded. He looked around slowly, as if to get his bearings.

"Just what I needed—a goddamn goat rodeo. I'll have your ass hauled off to Hays you so much as whisper Leonard Moye's name in your sleep."

Kevin nodded again, on the verge of tears, and watched Prance drive off.

He wiped his face and walked a block, then came to his own street, where at that late hour men still drank liquor on row-house stoops. They watched Kevin pass. He kept his eyes averted. Nothing about the street seemed real to him. No one spoke. It was as if he had died too, back there in Leonard Moye's field.

When he thought about William dropping in the barn, the back of his head erupting like an uncorked bottle of champagne, Kevin broke into an awkward run. To home and bed.

To lie restlessly with Leonard's eyes on him.

Maya slammed the bedroom door. Her knees gave out as she slumped to the floor. She cried, a jag that hurt her physically, pain in her rib cage, and breastbone sore.

A black paw appeared in the gap under the door. Maya watched the paw searching inches from her face on the floor. When Maya let in the cat, Miss Annie meowed as if offering thanks and curled into her lap.

"You little bitch," Maya said, rubbing the cat's scruff. "Almost got me killed."

She heard Leonard outside and prayed there were no more men out there coming to get her. Maya's ears were ringing.

Moments later there was a soft glow against the window. Maya got up, back against the wall, the cat in her arms. She walked slowly to the window. Parted a curtain and looked out at the fire burning near the barn.

She watched the fire for a while, saw Leonard as he circled a freshly dug pit, the lever-action rifle slung from a shoulder. At one point he looked at the house, as if aware of her watching him.

Her tears had stopped, dread replaced by a new feeling of solace and security.

Leonard flicked a cigarette onto the pyre.

Who he was cremating Maya couldn't say. But she knew it was over with.

For now.

She met him in the middle of the kitchen. When Maya started to sob, Leonard put his arms around her. She felt to him very much like a child, vulnerable, a pawn in the world of treachery and violence.

"I can feel your heart racing," she said.

"I'm wore out," he said. "Can't catch my breath."

"Is it all over now?"

"I think so."

He hadn't given much thought to Maya's secret, what it meant to the men determined to kill her.

Maya was still holding on to him when he said, "Tomorrow I want to show you something. It's important."

He looked down at her small shapely head; small enough he could palm her skull in his hand. Something stirred within him. Unaccustomed warmth. It occurred to Leonard that it had been a long time since he had even touched another human being.

He let Maya go, offering her a clean cloth to wipe away the tears. Then Leonard turned to the stove, anticipating that, like him, she had worked up an appetite from this short night of death and, for her perhaps, a measure of retribution.

EIGHT

THE SAME DAY DISPATCH RADIOED Jack Chalmers about smoke rising above the woods near Leonard's property, The Mayor had his tongue down the throat of a sloe-eyed runaway named Nikki. As he had requested, she had a dark complexion and a delicate frame on the verge of womanhood.

But she was no Maya.

They were in a suite at the Four Seasons in midtown. The Mayor was relaxing after a busy afternoon that had included the swearing-in of the new Fire & Rescue chief, a speech at a well-publicized summit on crime and the opening of a new cultural center near Inman Park.

He made Nikki lie down on her side and cozied up to her body, a hand beneath the black evening dress she wore.

The Mayor whispered in her ear and she giggled. Nikki was compliant and eager to please.

But she was no Maya.

He produced a small bottle of perfume, dabbed a little on her wrists and neck.

"This belonged to my foster mother," he had told her.

He asked Nikki how many clients she had been with. She wasn't supposed to talk about other men, but The Mayor told her it was fine, that her secrets were safe with him. Lucio wouldn't punish her, because *he* was the boss, after all.

When Nikki closed her eyes he wondered if she was remembering other men.

All he thought about was Maya.

While Nikki undressed, The Mayor locked himself in the bathroom. In the magnified makeup mirror he was shocked by his reflection. Lack of sleep was apparent, worry lines around his eyes. He undressed and put on a robe with the hotel's monogram, then removed a few items from his toiletry kit.

The girl was naked on the bed, posing like a garden nymph, when The Mayor reappeared. She glanced over her shoulder, smiling professionally. He let the robe fall open as he walked to the bed. Tossed an unwrapped condom to her and smiled. The girl rolled over on her back.

She swept the hair out of her eyes and when she looked saw the syringe in his other hand.

Eric Lambert was annoyed by the message on his phone. Call for a meeting with Lucio. Meaning something was wrong. He checked his watch, and then banged on the bedroom door of the suite. A few moments later The Mayor answered through the door.

"Almost done here," he said, breathing hard.

After a couple of minutes the bedroom door opened. Lambert pushed past The Mayor, who was belting himself into the robe.

The girl sat on the edge of the bed, wrapped in a bedsheet, mascara streaky on her cheeks. She looked dazed.

"What did you give her?"

"The usual."

"Hey," Lambert said to the girl, pinching her chin. "Come on."

Her eyes were unfocused. She fell over when Lambert gave her a push.

"Can you get dressed?"

Nikki wiped her mouth with the back of a hand and nodded. Lambert figured that at least the girl wouldn't remember any of it, only that vague sense of debasement, and the injury, of course. He pulled her to her feet and started her toward the bathroom. Followed with her overnight bag. He closed the door.

"Don't lock it," Lambert told her.

The Mayor had parted curtains and was watching a hearse drive slowly east on 14th Street. He could see the distant promenade, a balloon floating above a row of dogwoods, catching a breeze and drifting away. Below him in the street three kids sold bottled water near a bus stop, the huddled bodies of homeless men, supine on benches nearby. A police car, followed by an ambulance, appeared and sped past the men, announcing to the city that somebody's ticket had probably been punched.

Four miles away, looking south to City Hall, was the looming high-rise. A construction crane lifted steel beams into the air.

"Remind me to order blinds or everybody in that skyscraper will be able to see into my office."

"We've got a problem."

The Mayor smiled.

"She'll be fine."

"Not that."

"Maya?"

"Probably. No details yet."

The Mayor closed his eyes. Looking pained, he pressed his hand to the window.

"Well, where is she?"

"Our friends from Tamaulipas are now getting curious. Chatter about Lucio having a snitch among his crew. That murdered cop was a client working both sides of the street."

"But I thought Lucio handled that."

"He did. But Maya apparently talked to him. Dead men tell tales sometimes."

"But isn't she——?"

"Still alive."

"Still?"

"It's time I took care of it."

"You know I don't want her to suffer, Eric."

"She won't."

Lambert wanted to slap him, if anything for that sorry tone of voice. He had had enough of this bird on the wing and didn't care how she died. The Mayor could fantasize about peaceful endings and sunlight through church windows.

"I've got an exploratory committee to address," he said, as if reminding Lambert that too many distractions were detrimental to his political effectiveness.

"You're told the stove is hot and yet you keep touching it."

The Mayor shrugged. The bathroom door opened. Nikki was dressed in a matching sweat suit, looking okay but still adrift. Lambert left his boss standing at the window and led her to the private elevator in the foyer.

Two of Lucio's men waited in a black sport utility in the hotel's parking garage. Lambert handed the girl off and went back upstairs.

The Mayor was in the suite's living room, dressed in dinner clothes, watching himself on the six o'clock news. Lambert sat at a conference table, poured a cup of coffee from room service. He opened a laptop and looked over a property map.

"What are you looking at?" The Mayor said.

"You should know. You and Lucio own most of it now."

"I don't own anything."

"My mistake."

"Eric, could you let Maya know that I—?"

Lambert let the question hang for a moment before answering.

"Of course, sir," he said, tracing the interstate with a finger south to Trickum County. "I'll give her your best wishes."

Chalmers drove toward the rising smoke on Leonard's property.

He had had to stop once already to move a windfall. With the prowler's A/C on the fritz Chalmers was sweating profusely, the stains spreading across his forest-green uniform shirt to the beltline.

He passed a shallow, scummed-over pond, its edges rimmed with hawthorn and cyrilla. On the widening clay road, Chalmers noted tire tracks. From Leonard's Studebaker, he guessed.

The road abruptly hooked left, and he crossed the pond by way of a plank bridge. He looked down at the water, wondering what would happen to the cruiser if those planks gave way.

But the bridge held. A lone palmetto marked the beginning of cleared acreage in the midst of those woods. He turned onto the dirt track and followed it a half mile into thick timber, noted the dozens of posted signs tacked to tree trunks, a warning to trespassers. Eventually he came to a pasture, a sea of wheat and wild grass rolling away and down until he saw the scarecrows. His radio crackled.

"Chalmers, Prance here. What's your 20?"

Chalmers keyed the mic.

"I'm investigating a possible Signal 33 out by the paper company."

"Copy that, Chalmers. Call was unfounded. There's no fire. Resume normal traffic."

"10-4," Chalmers radioed back, thinking, *the hell I will.*

He drove on, admiring the refuge Leonard had created for him-self. Both bay doors were closed on the big tobacco barn, eaves on either side of the roof providing a trim of shade. There was a wind-mill next to an elevated tank, the shaft and gears drawing water from the ground. Leonard then used simple gravity to bring run-ning water into the house. Probably not enough pressure to take a shower, but it would do, Chalmers thought. A reminder, too, that Leonard belonged to an era that produced very capable men, born with the kind of common sense most city folk paid other people to have nowadays.

Chalmers parked his Crown Vic near the chicken coop in the yard. Hibiscus thrived in a large wild garden fronting the house. A few purple martins fussed around the gourd poles. He saw Leonard out near a stand of pines, leaning on a shovel, watching a fire line inch away from him.

Leonard looked his way and regarded him suspiciously. Chalmers hesitated by the cedar tree, noticing the disturbed earth and a glint on the ground. He toed the brass shell casing, then picked it up and put it in his pocket before glancing at the house once more. He wondered where that Studebaker was, the stills, certain there must be some good whiskey still buried on that land somewhere.

And that damn mannequin that filled him with pity.

He walked toward Leonard. The old man dipped a tin cup into a pitcher and brought it to his lips. Ran a sleeve across his mouth. He saw the holster on Leonard's right hip and the Marlin leaning against a trash barrel.

Leonard had not changed in the years since Chalmers had been a deputy. A tall, lean man whom even in the harsh afternoon light and despite his gray hair still looked to be in his prime. Leonard acknowledged Chalmers, turned to drive his spade into the soil, scooping dirt onto flame getting away from him.

"Jack," he said.

"Been a while," Chalmers said, and tipped the brim of his campaign hat.

"Is there a problem?"

"I figure you must've forgot you need a permit for a prescribed burn."

"Must have," Leonard said. He leaned slightly but alertly on his shovel. Chalmers kept his distance.

"Got a report this morning of smoke over this way."

"Considering it's damn near three in the afternoon I see you were in a hurry to investigate."

"This place isn't exactly easy to find. How long have you been at it?"

"Since I noticed some brown spot in them pines. Aim to seed another stand of longleaf come fall."

"Odd time for a burn, wouldn't you say?"

Leonard made a face. "Nothing odd about it."

Chalmers sparred eyes with the old man and, realizing he was losing, looked back at the field.

"Your daddy?" Leonard said.

"Sick. Quit smoking and put the bottle down for good last I heard, but it's too little, too late. You of all people should know how difficult that must've been."

"Never tasted the stuff," Leonard said. "Whiskey was made to sell, not drink."

"Why you were so good at your trade, I imagine."

Leonard wiped sweat from his forehead.

"Anything else I can do for you?"

"Just here about the smoke is all." Chalmers pointed to the pistol at Leonard's hip. "You do much shooting out here?"

"Just at the law."

Chalmers's expression darkened, and Leonard laughed at what he must have seen and threw another shovel of dirt on his crawling fire.

"You should see your face, boy," he said.

Chalmers reached into his pocket and showed the shell casing to Leonard.

"Picked this up yonder. Nine-millimeter. That a caliber you prefer?"

Leonard's gaze settled on the casing before he looked past Chalmers at the house.

"Got me one of them *semis* at a trade show. Italian piece. No kick to it. Was popping off a few rounds last night."

"That would explain the report of gunfire," Chalmers said.

"It would."

"You still live out here by yourself?"

Leonard shook his head.

"Me and my wife. You know that."

Chalmers nodded.

"I forgot. And how *is* Marjean?"

"Fine." Leonard said, unsmiling. "She's inside."

Chalmers sucked his bottom lip to keep from saying what was really on his mind.

"You know I saw you in town."

"I get out there from time to time. Wanting to pick up a few things," Leonard said.

His stare plainly indicated he didn't like the question, and wanted Chalmers gone. Something was going on here, Chalmers thought, in this isolated place, that he hadn't caught hold of yet.

"You and Marjean have any visitors?"

"No. We don't ever have company—anymore. Reckon that be all, *Deputy?*"

"For now," Chalmers said.

After a spell of silence he realized he wasn't going to get anywhere. Chalmers walked back to his patrol car, curious about those size 6 footprints in the sand, and also that second tin cup near Leonard's pitcher.

The one still beaded with condensation.

Maya had brought Leonard the pitcher of cold water, feeling worried as she watched him pat down with his shovel the charred earth where Gregory Grimes and William Watkins had lain a half hour earlier. An acre of grass and brush had been scorched so far. Leonard tended his burn line carefully, the smolder rising in thick ribbons. He had buried the remains of the most recent trespassers, with the hope that scavengers wouldn't come along and dig them up. No trace of the bodies remained for now, however, nor any indication Leonard had dug the graves, either. Maya saw sweat dripping from his brow. It occurred to Maya that all this effort had been for her sake, but when he looked her way all he had to say was, "What did you do to them jeans?"

Maya smiled bashfully. The surgery she had performed with Marjean's sewing scissors had resulted in frayed cutoffs, reasonably comfortable given the temperature and stylish, if she didn't mind to think so herself. She bent down, picked at a scab on a kneecap, licked a fingertip, and dabbed the scratch gone bloody.

"Too hot out here to wear mama jeans, Leonard."

"*Mama* jeans?"

"Kind you tuck up under your titties," Maya said.

"You know you got legs like a bird?"

"Well, there's men paid good money for these legs to be company for a night."

Leonard's face went flush.

"Don't talk like that."

"You know, for a badass, Leonard, you sure are a prude."

She laughed and then took off in a sprint across the grass. Leonard watched her skip, then vault sideways into a cartwheel, all limbs and hair suddenly wild as a pinwheel, the white bottoms of her feet flashing. But she couldn't stick the landing and bounced with a thud onto her butt.

Leonard clapped.

"Most of that was pretty impressive."

Maya tied her hair back. Held up a finger to signal another attempt was imminent and, steadying herself, vaulted back across the grass into a double cartwheel that sent birds flying into the air. This time she ended up with a clumsy two-footed hop, her arms upflung like those of an Olympic hopeful.

Leonard applauded the effort, too.

"Where did you learn that?"

"A girl from Russia I knew," Maya said. "Taught me gymnastics."

"Where at?"

Maya began dancing playfully where the grass gave way to warm, chalk-colored sand.

"Place they kept us was like a dormitory," she said. "When we had some playtime we used to somersault down the halls."

Leonard tried to picture it but couldn't get a grip on the arrangement she had been subject to. He watched her feet, tapping heel-toe into a twirl.

"How many girls are we talking about?"

"Ten or so," she said. "Sometimes more. Girls came and went. Lucio moved us around a lot, too. Traveled in limousines. Even did it in the back of one."

Lenard gestured that he had heard enough.

Maya ignored his displeasure. She pirouetted, raising her arms like a ballerina in fifth position.

"Mainly did it in hotels though," she said. "Fancy suites. Other times just quickies in the afternoon while the wife was getting her hair done. Clients paid to Lucio's legit businesses. One guy made me wear a wedding dress once. There was another, big shot from Washington, DC, he liked his girls wearing Pampers."

Maya giggled but Leonard shook his head in disgust.

"How did he get away with this?"

"Lucio hid a lot of money," she said. "And he kept a lot of dirt on people, including cops. Used it to lord over them in case they wanted to snitch him out. Was last year when he set me up with *The Mayor*. Said I was on retainer, his only girl. They're like, like partners, you see."

"So that's him, huh? The famous one?"

"Yeah," Maya said.

"And they're partners? In what?"

"Working with a big drug cartel like I said, to buy up a bunch of land down here. And the cartel is going to invest in his campaign when he runs for governor."

"My God. Where around here?"

Maya told him.

"That's twenty thousand acres of timber. What are they going to do with it?"

"Underground labs where they can cook the drugs and move it."

She rattled off some numbers, tonnage, and price points.

"You remember all that detail?"

Maya nodded.

"I don't forget a face or a name either. It's all up here."

Leonard's eyes narrowed in anger.

Neither of them spoke for a while. Maya watched two cats atop a rusted water pump take turns whacking each other on the head. Another one, pregnant and with a belly so swollen it was dragging on the ground, disappeared into the shadow of the toolshed.

"So that's my story," Maya said.

"So Mr. Mayor. He the one gave you the brand on your shoulder?"

"Uh-huh."

"Have a name?"

She told him.

"I can't believe it."

"He thinks he's going be president one day. He and Lucio are like half brothers."

"How's that?"

"They were orphans. Adopted, right? But Lucio told me they had the same mother. Don't know how he found that out or if it's even true."

Leonard dipped a tin cup into the pitcher Maya had brought and handed it to her. His hand shook. Water spilled.

"Take a sip."

Maya swallowed two big gulps. She pressed her knees together.

"Got to pee."

Leonard nodded and leaned on the shovel, absently staring at the burn line. He thought about the dead men on his land, and the nature of secrets, his, Maya's, those of the three corpses he'd created, human mysteries buried in the muck of incomprehensible lives.

Normal to some, he reminded himself, *is crazy to others.*

Leonard decided then he had to tell Maya the truth, as he knew it.

Maya's impulse on hearing the approach of the police cruiser was to duck out of sight.

She peeked through the window above the kitchen sink, heart pounding as the patrol car appeared and parked beside the chicken coop. The deputy got out and stood in the shade of the big cedar tree for a moment, looking around.

Maya slipped like a shadow into the living room and crouched beside Marjean. The deputy walked across the yard, moving toward Leonard and the burn line.

Maya looked up at the mannequin and whispered.

"You got any ideas I'd love to hear 'em."

If the deputy was asking to come into the house, for whatever reason, then she could hide in the closet or maybe the crawl space. Even with the lock broken it still was the best place. Chillbumps spread on Maya's arms as an awful scenario played out in her mind.

What if Leonard shoots him?

Got to expect it, girl, she thought.

So what do you do?

Maya imagined herself shoveling dirt onto a man in uniform near the carcass of a burned-out patrol car.

Drawn to Maya in her anxiety, the black cat rubbed against her leg and purred.

"Quiet, Miss Annie."

Maya snapped out of her fearful daydream and watched anxiously as Leonard and the police officer talked, Leonard looking a bit hostile but still calm and collected. The deputy was tall and physically fit. Handsome, Maya thought. There was a faint resemblance between the deputy and Leonard, too. She got to her feet and moved away from Marjean, back to the wall now. The deputy approached the house again. He had his hand on the driver's-side door when he turned for a last, speculative look at the house.

She was afraid to move. But the deputy finally got into the cruiser and drove away.

Leonard found her in the bedroom, standing over a lift-top sewing table that had belonged to his grandmother. Atop it was a sewing machine made of cast iron, with a hand crank, the foundry marks inside the wheel castings dating the machine to the last century. Maya wiped her cheeks, hooked a strand of hair behind an ear. Leonard wondered about her interest in the old sewing machine.

"He's gone, if that's why you're upset."

"Was it me he was here about?"

"Some fool saw the smoke from the highway and called the law."

"I thought you were going to shoot him."

Leonard chuckled.

"Why? Because I seem to shoot everyone else comes around here?"

But his attempt at humor fell flat. Maya looked away. She ran a finger along the sewing machine's tensioner.

"What is this thing?"

"Ever seen a stitch machine before? Been in my family a long time. Marjean sewed her own dresses on it, like a hobby."

"She did?"

Leonard nodded.

"Come with me," he said. "Got somethin' to show you."

He motioned to a blanket chest at the foot of the bed and opened the lid. The original varnish was crackled, the surface imbued with green and black streaks. The interior had been lined with old newspaper. There was a stack of cotton dresses inside the chest.

"You can have any you want," he said.

Maya held up the first dress, a full-length blue affair with poufy sleeves and a scoop neckline.

"I'll be right back."

She tucked and rolled the skirt so it wouldn't drag, pinched the fit around her torso so the dress didn't hang. Marjean had been taller, full-framed, but Maya loved the pattern. She thought with some scissor work she could make an elegant sundress from Marjean's creation.

She returned from the bathroom, handfuls of cloth pulled here and there to show Leonard how the dress would fit with alterations.

She looked expectantly at Leonard. He nodded with approval.

"I don't know much about women," he said. "But I do know they like a nice dress."

"That they do," Maya said and smiled. "Marjean got any safety pins?"

Leonard carried the mannequin to the bed and opened the curtains, allowing full sun into the normally dim room. He excused himself and shut the door, figuring Marjean would want to help Maya make the dress her own.

Forty-five minutes later she called to him.

He opened the armoire, noting Maya's expression when she saw the rifles and shotguns racked where clothes should go. A blotchy, spotted mirror hung from one of the doors. Maya turned this way and that, admiring the recreated dress in the mirror, then looked back at Marjean as if she might have something to add. The mannequin had tipped over onto its side, lying on the bed like something from the store that needed returning.

Leonard righted the mannequin and nodded his approval to Maya.

"Fit for church, I'd say."

"I feel better," she said. "A nice dress can make a girl feel better. How about you?"

"Meaning?"

"What makes you feel better, Leonard?"

Leonard selected a Stevens double-barrel from the gun rack. He snapped opened the breech, removed two shells from his pocket and slid them in.

"This always does the trick. Say we go for a walk?"

"That a good idea, Leonard?"

But he was already gone, leading the way with his shotgun.

The sky was flushed as they walked toward the clearing, Maya barefoot and surprised to enjoy the feel of dirt between her toes. The scarecrows were less intimidating in this shadowless light. Maya took a strange liking to them, as if they were part of a larger army that included Leonard and Marjean protecting her. The field a kind of sanctuary she had never known.

Leonard told her how he had cleared the land on his own, brute labor every acre of it. His daddy raised corn, but cotton was his main crop. A bale of cotton could weigh four or five hundred pounds, Leonard said, bringing—in good times—maybe four cents a pound. They raised pigs, too. Cows and some goats.

"Things were a lot different when I was your age," he said. "My daddy would spread our meat on top of the corn in a log crib, corn shucks soaking up the all the salt so the cows would fatten sooner. My grandmamma, you would have liked her. She would cord sheep's wool and spin it on an old spinning wheel, making clothes for me."

"Life was hard back then?"

"It was what it was. You just deal with what's in front of you. Folks a hundred years from now will probably complain all the same. The world will never stop being incomprehensible."

Leonard stopped to light a cigarette. He and Maya stood in the shade of a white oak at the northeast corner of the field.

"Tell me more," Maya said. "About your life."

"Okay," he said. "So Christmas was always the best time of year. Put my daddy in a good mood. He would give us fifty-cent pieces, tell us to go on into town and treat ourselves. We'd wake up on Christmas morning to apples, raisins, and peppermint candy."

Maya fingered the bark of the oak tree. A crude heart had been carved into the trunk. Leonard watched her for a moment before his reminiscences turned to Marjean.

"Where did you two meet?" she said.

"In school. I remember this old shed used to be an outhouse, and at recess a few of the girls would run down to it and crowd inside, to gossip and giggle and such. They wouldn't play with us boys, so one night me and my pals raised the back of the outhouse and took the block out and propped it up. Next day at school the girls ran like usual to the shed and crowded in until their weight tipped it over backward."

"What did the girls do?"

Leonard smiled.

"A whole lot of screaming and hollering. Marjean was the first to climb out. She saw me laughing like a fool with the other boys. She walked right up to us, but singled me out, and then punched me in the nose."

"She hit you?"

"She did. While I stood there bleeding, I knew I was in love."

Maya grew quiet as she followed Leonard toward the center of the field, listening as he told her more stories from his youth. She twirled a flower between her fingers and watched him with a muted fondness.

"So how did you start making liquor?"

"I was eighteen and working at a garage over in Miller County. One day this fella brought his car in to be worked on, said he was looking to drive a load of stolen booze up north and needed a mechanic, in case anything happened to the car on the road. Paid me two hundred dollars for the run to Huntsville. No trouble with the law and it was easy money. I was hooked."

"That's all you did?" she said.

"Oh, I worked straight jobs. Mechanic, fixing farm equipment, driving a taxi, you name it. But that outlaw life was fun. Trickum was a dry county for a long time, and there was money to be made here. Folks loved them that tax-free whiskey, didn't like having to go over to a wet county to buy it. Was a man owned a few pool halls and he sold black market whiskey in his joints. I used to drive deliveries for him, too. I got pretty good at trapping a car, rigging compartments to hide it."

"And you never got caught?"

Leonard shook his head.

"Had a close call near Thomasville but that was it. I used back roads far from the highways. Had routes with lookouts posted who would hit their horn if they saw the law. There was a whole network of service stations back then, too. If the sheriff got on us we could switch a trap car for a clean car in a hurry."

"I thought you said you made the whiskey yourself?"

Leonard stopped and watched a red-tailed hawk circling above the field.

"Eventually, I bought two copper stills and chopped up a Hudson, took out the back seats and put in steel tanks. I did it all. Charred and painted the barrels myself, then buried them in the woods. They never could find a one of my batches."

"You sure stuck it to those police, huh?"

"Ones I couldn't pay off, sure. It was like a game. They would walk every foot of my land. I'd say, 'You don't think I'm dumb enough to cache liquor then pave a road to it, do you?'"

"Where did you make the moon—?"

"Moonshine?"

He flashed a mischievous smile and pointed down at the ground.

"I built my still in the one place nobody had the nerve to venture into—the caves."

Maya listened to his grand history without interruption, attuned to his drawl and the timbre of his voice as much as the tales themselves.

At dusk they zigzagged among the scarecrows, watching for snakes as they crossed a swath of grass. With the shotgun in the crook of his arm, Leonard paused to admire the rising moon. They heard a doe snort and crash off toward the woods. There was a long silence as if his brain had been exhausted by his unusual talkativeness.

"You make a lot of money," Maya said. "Selling the alcohol?"

"I made enough," he said. "Never could see the idea of working for money, then throwing it away."

"Who did the buying?"

"Sold my stuff to a lot to dance halls, backcountry bars, and gambling dens. Used to call them speakeasies or blind pigs way back in the days of Prohibition but that was before my time. I had regulars, too. Bought it by the gallon. They waited on themselves."

"Like a self-service?"

"Yeah. I had holes dug alongside the roads and all my customers knew where *their* jug was buried. Thing was, no one knew where the others were. When they wanted a gallon they would drive to that hole at night and pick it up. I'd walk down the roads and if one was gone, I would replace it that night, take out my little ledger and charge it to them. Call by their office or home to collect my money."

"What you do with all that money? You buy Marjean nice things? Go on trips?"

He shrugged.

"We never did without, but I don't trust any bank worth a damn. So mostly I just buried it."

"*Buried* money?"

Leonard did not elaborate.

They finally arrived at the two gravestones side by side. Maya heard a thrum on the air and watched a colony of bats scatter across the sky like a round of birdshot.

She knelt beside the smaller of the two markers. The engraving was crudely rendered and nearly illegible. She traced a finger over the stone and looked up at Leonard.

"You and Marjean had a baby?" she said.

He looked as though he was about to nod but held his gaze on the headstones and then told Maya the story.

Annie was born in the summertime. Had me a Chevy 210, and I drove the wheels off it getting Marjean to Linette Kurbo's house. She was a midwife that lived in a crossroads town by the name of Climax. I helped Marjean inside and saying, I'll go for a walk now, just holler when it's done, and I hit the road, stepping around clods of horseshit. Walked circles around that house till past midnight when Linette stuck her head out a window and yelled my name. The baby was healthy, had all her fingers and toes and we both liked the name Annabelle but Annie for short so that's what we named her then and there.

Marjean wasn't right, though. First few months after Annie was born she hardly slept and I had to force her to eat. Started to have fits, a temper like I'd never seen before. Threatening to call the law on me. She would turn cold when I put my hand on her. Then things she used to do like work the garden, plant peppers and tomatoes, make her quilts and housedresses, none of that seemed to matter much. She wasn't the same woman. But I thought it would pass.

I remember how that week had its sights on me and there was no place to hide. Just ill omens everywhere. Started with this nasty bulldog belonged to Judge Boyett, who was a customer of mine. He had the kind of dog that could chew a man to pieces. Supposed to be chained up in the backyard. So after midnight I eased in the gate and set the basket of liquor in the rocking chair on his porch and what do I hear then but that damn bulldog, comin' around the house with a block and chain around its neck. I just did make it out of the yard. Dog tore my pants leg when I jumped the fence.

Then the next day I was driving back from the river and picked up hitchhikers. One of 'em tried to bust my head with a jack handle. I had a

.38 in a leather case strapped to the steering post, and I shot him in the ass and left the sorry lot of them on the side of the road.

Following night I found out a boy who delivered for me owed money all over town so I had to pay his debts then got a hold of him and beat him until he couldn't walk. Not proud of it now, but that's the way things were done back then. For a little while I went legit and owned a café with a small dance hall. That Thursday a son of a bitch tried to wreck the place so I had to teach him that the public didn't run my place, I ran the public, so I hit him with an axe handle a few times, then I handcuffed him and threw him off a bridge. He waded ashore but his elbows never worked right after that.

I look back, Maya, and wonder if maybe there were signs I should of paid closer mind to.

Because Friday afternoon that week I came home after being up all night and Marjean was in the yard digging in her garden. First I thought how nice it was to see her doing something she loved again. But when I asked her 'bout the baby she made a face I didn't like. I asked her again and she laughed, not at me exactly, but at some notion only she found funny. I knew something was bad wrong.

I rushed inside the house and found Annabelle's body lying on the bed.

Marjean had smothered our baby girl until she stopped moving and put her inside a feed sack. Tied it off with a miller's knot. Figure she had been dead a few hours.

So I untied the knot and pulled Annie's body out of the sack and held her. She was colder than anything I had ever touched. Skin was blue. Kept wanting her to move or make a sound but she wouldn't. I'd seen death plenty different ways but something about my own flesh and blood made the hurt so much worse. Them little fingers and toes of hers. I can still picture them.

I walked outside with Annie's body, back to the garden, where Marjean was on her knees, rocking back and forth, the front of her dress soiled like she had been playing in the dirt. She was trying with her bare hands to dig a hole big enough for the baby. I asked her why and she told me she didn't know but she just wasn't fit and I said you're damn right but I started to cry because this was the woman I loved so dearly and she had betrayed me. Then she told me she loved me and Annie more than anything on earth and that God would forgive her one day and I said God would forgive you momentarily and I raised the pistol in my other hand, and before some sensible impulse could cause me to reconsider I shot Marjean through the head.

Maya wiped tears from her eyes. Then she hugged him.

"Do you believe me?" Leonard said, his voice shaky.

Leonard felt her nod and she squeezed him tighter. He kissed the top of her head. There was still a lot of hurt, but no longer the torment, even if what he had told Maya was all a lie.

Say sister I hope you can find our way.
—U. S. Christmas, "Say Sister"

NINE

"I work alone," Lambert said. "Nonnegotiable."

Lucio looked up from his meal of pad thai but said nothing. He and Lambert were an hour south of the city, inside a contractor trailer near Atlanta Motor Speedway. Race teams down from Charlotte were testing and the powerful motors caused the trailer to vibrate slightly as the stock cars bunched down the front stretch. Lambert's attention shifted to a bald-headed man too tall to stand upright in the trailer. He peeked between window blinds with a scissoring of his fingers, scanning the clay lot outside. Lambert glimpsed I-beams and earthmovers. A surveyor looked up from his transit and studied the horizon as if it were about to vanish.

"The dead narc has caused some heat," Lucio said. "I want to placate our friends from the south."

He reached for a bottle of lotion and rubbed a teaspoon's worth into the tattoo on his forearm.

"You should be worried," Lambert said. "We all should."

"You ever have been to Matamoros? I'm sure some of your Blackwelder buddies have."

"I've been all over."

"Then you know the nature of our partners. How they solve their problems? How they relieve their doubts?"

Lambert shrugged indifferently.

"She's just a whore. What's the worst that could happen?"

"Maya walks into an agency—pick one—with a head full of wild stories and somebody takes her seriously," Lucio said. "He did tell her *everything*, after all."

"How do you know that?"

"The girl is a human tape recorder. But that didn't stop me from planting a bug on Maya from time to time. And not my fault The Mayor's idea of pillow talk is describing a complex criminal enterprise to a piece of ass."

"You greasy little shit."

Lucio leaned back in his chair and smiled.

"I got dirt on everybody. A guaranteed *get out of jail free* card. What is it with him? Is he in love with her? Is that it?"

"That's enough."

"Things get anymore sideways, we won't live to see the fruits of our labor," Lucio said. "And His Honor knows campaigns cost money—a lot of money."

"He's confident in our arrangement."

"Did you know Gulf hitters have a penchant for skinning, scalping, and arranging genitalia on sidewalks like floral tributes? The fact of the matter is these boys in the snakeskin boots are antsy, but they have always wanted to own a state governor. His Honor's judgment is clouded, however. He needs to get over it, and we need to give them Maya's head in a bucket."

"It's time I take care of this business." Lambert said.

"*We* take care of it, now."

Lucio stood and gestured to the rifle bag on the floor. His driver grabbed it and then opened the door of the trailer. Lambert followed them outside to a waiting Ford Bronco with four-wheel drive. They

left just as a late summer storm overtook the racetrack, plumes of red
dust kicking into the air.

The places had biblical-sounding names—*Megiddo, Damascus,
Herod*—one-stop towns potholed and beaten to death under a mer-
ciless sun. Despite the warm weather Lambert had worn his blazer,
concealing the snubbie in the small of his back and the SIG Sauer
semiauto in a leather pancake holster. *Two is one and one is none.*
There was a change of clothes in the trunk. A rifle bag containing
his M21 and match ammo.

The gasoline had been Lucio's idea.

They passed roadside vendors advertising bait and tackle, produce stands with boiled peanuts, melons and lettuce and squash for
sale. Countless service stations, many of them abandoned. Baptist
churches. Cemeteries housing the Confederate dead. Creeks the
color of weak coffee. Roadkill. At one point they came upon a poul-
try plant, a sulfuric smell that filled the air. Lambert figured that to
the locals it smelled like home.

Finally they arrived in Trickum, cruising through its
postcard-perfect square, past the courthouse and live oaks bearded
with bromeliad, a coffee shop, the beauty parlor, an antique store,
the gazebo and stage where the high school marching band
would perform "Glory, Glory Dixieland" prior to the homecom-
ing game. But Lucio and Lambert didn't linger and headed on
toward the eastern edge of the county. No shortage of raw land
out there, state wilderness and undeveloped timber as far as the
eye could see, land that for some families was their most precious
possession yet more often than not were quick to sell when it
came to cash money.

Lucio's driver slowed to read a mile marker, followed by a sign for a boat landing. A few minutes later he hung a left onto a logging road marked by newly tacked No TRESPASSING signs. Lambert looked out at rows and rows of planted pine trees, aware of the holding companies and trusts that had bought up tract after tract, always cash. To the people down here the entities buying up land appeared unrelated, with their nominee owners and registered agents. The only attention these transactions received were editorials in the *Trickum Searchlight*, written by an area mortgage broker praising the effectiveness of private conservation when conservation proceedings had failed at the state and federal level.

Meanwhile, the cotton farmers kept growing their cotton. The roofers went on roofing. The drinkers drank and the preachers preached. Unknown to them all that much of Trickum County had been sold to the snakeskin boys from Tamaulipas.

The road dipped and climbed through a wooded acreage and was hell on the SUV's suspension. When they arrived at the pond, Ronnie Prance was waiting for them, looking hot and bothered and fanning the air as if under siege. There was a portable storage shed a few yards away. Weeds and shoreland plants grew thick along the banks of the pond, and Prance glanced nervously at a rustling in the overgrowth.

"Humidity got you looking ugly?" Lucio said.

"Took long enough. Goddamn air conditioner quit on me," Prance said.

Lucio pointed to the revolver on Prance's hip.

"As if you've ever fired that relic."

"Damn near had to the other night when your boys got barbecued."

Lucio gestured to Lambert.

"He'll be fixing our problem now."

Prance looked him up and down.

"What? No name?" he said.

Lambert smiled, regarding Prance with a cool superiority.

Prance sucked one last long drag on his cigarette before dropping it at his feet.

"So let me guess. You're a big-time ass kicker here to handle this bootlegger. I bet you shave twice a day and bounce a nickel off your bedspread every morning. What are you? Ex-military?"

"I'm good with people," Lambert said.

Prance looked back at the pond. Sniffed the air.

"Something spook you?"

"Hear that grunting? Seen a gator in there the size of a Buick. Reckon he knows the cooks just arrived."

On cue Lambert walked past him to the shed. Cracked the door. Inside he saw a cordless saw, assorted cutting tools, butcher's paper, a drop cloth, five-gallon buckets, and a few bottles of bleach. He whistled, glanced back at Lucio.

"Anyone bound to be out this way?"

"Leonard's place abuts some public land but bowhunting season is still a few weeks away, so it's doubtful." Prance said. He lit another cigarette and leaned against his car, flashing a snide smile.

"Game warden?"

"Happens to be a pal of mine," Prance said. "He's smart enough to know doing the right thing and living to be proud of it are often mutually exclusive. He'll stay out of the way—for now."

He reached inside his car for a Coca-Cola, peanuts floating in the bottle. Took a sip, followed by a satisfied breath.

"So what's the plan?"

The men exchanged glances. Lambert drummed his fingers against a canister of gasoline. Lucio told him.

Then Prance put a hand on the hood of his car to steady himself.

Maya let out a whoop when the Studebaker stalled and then jerked forward with a groan. She mashed the throttle and yanked the wheel again. Leonard sat beside her, barking instructions—*Clutch! Shift! Gas! Brake!*—as Maya downshifted, letting out the clutch, her feet dancing on the pedals.

The sedan slowed while Maya concentrated on following tire tracks made during previous laps around the house. Terrified cats watched from the limb of a cedar tree. Leonard cringed when he heard the gears grinding. Could smell exhaust as the Studebaker slid to a stop a few feet before Maya could add a new bay door to the barn.

Then the engine died.

Red dust settled around them.

Maya let go of the shifter knob, threw her arms around Leonard's neck and kissed his cheek. He blushed as she clapped in excitement.

"How'd I do, Leonard? How'd I do?"

"I'd say you done killed her."

He laughed and then opened the door and got out. Circled the Studebaker as if at any moment it might begin telling him its symptoms. The car had a metallic beige body faded with age and sun. The once whitewall tires were caked with dirt but still in decent shape.

Leonard raised the hood, fanning smoke that billowed from the engine. He had always hoarded parts and had an irrational fear of engines becoming obsolete, not a drive shaft or oil valve to be found one day.

It didn't take long for Leonard to determine the best fate for the old Studebaker—a solemn burial in the Flint River.

"Did I break it?" Maya said.

He shook his head sorrowfully, but there was humor in his eyes.

"Ol' gal has seen a lot of road in her day," he said. "Finally met her match."

Leonard wiped his brow with a handkerchief and smiled. Since Maya's arrival, part of him had let go of that fixation on the past and his peculiar values and possessions, and his hermetic way of life. The girl was reason for him to take stock, to consider a long-overdue accounting of where he stood in the timestream of his life.

Maya got out and walked alongside the car.

"Is that a bullet hole?" she said, pointing to, then fingering the perforation in the Studebaker's right front panel.

Leonard nodded and passed a hand over the right rear well.

"That one there was buckshot."

"Who shot at you? The cops?"

"Marjean."

"She shot at you?"

Leonard shrugged.

"It's how we used to argue."

"What happened?"

"Long time ago, I used to drive the owner of a sawmill around town. Man's wife had taken a liking to this fella from Alabama that played a pool-hall twelve-string guitar for nickels. Good-looking scoundrel. Kid picked that thing and women would pass that pool hall just to watch him, Marjean among them. But the sawmill boss didn't like his wife paying attention to a handsome young buck like that. He gave me five dollars to run him out of town. So I drove down to the pool hall and there he was picking his guitar and I admit, it was quite a sight, all those women taken with him—Marjean right there with 'em. I walked over and said, '*Boy, I can pick that thing, too!*' He handed over the guitar like he was daring me to and I busted it over his head. The women just shrieked. The boy ran off into the woods with the guitar hanging around his neck and that's how

Marjean come to pull her .32 wheel gun from her purse and shot at me, yelling: '*Leonard, you son of a bitch, we were just enjoying and now he ain't got no guitar!*'"

"Was she really that mad?" Maya said.

"Mad enough to drive off in my car. So I had to walk home, and time I got back she was sitting out on the porch and this time she had my shotgun. She fired a warning shot. Aimed low but damn near blew off my big toe. To keep the peace I had to promise to buy that kid a new guitar."

"Did you?"

"With the five bucks I got paid to wreck it in the first place, along with a soda pop and—because Marjean had me feeling guilty about the whole thing—a bottle of liquor, besides. Those were crazy times."

"They're still crazy," Maya said.

He hesitated; time traveling in his eyes and frozen expression. Her voice brought him back.

"What's that?" he said.

"What color were your baby's eyes?" Maya said.

Leonard looked off.

"Well—I don't remember," he said.

"I bet she was beautiful."

He didn't answer, unable to meet Maya's gaze.

"So what makes babies go bad?" she said, as if to change the subject. "Why do they have to grow up and do terrible things to other people?"

"I don't know. Suppose there's a tradition of evil, gets carried on from generation to generation. Always been here, always will be. Them men that used you for money," he said. "They were all ugly, weren't they?"

"Just seems like I've never known a good person, Leonard. You're the first I ever known that wasn't that kind of ugly."

"I'm no saint," he said. "I've got my uglies, all right. Got a beak on me that'd make a hawk jealous. And just the other day I yanked a few gray hairs growing out my ears."

He laughed, but Maya's eyes had filled with emotion. She took a step toward Leonard.

He wanted to move away. But whatever reserve he had been holding on to left him with a sigh. He held out an arm to Maya, and they embraced and he told her that whatever happened to him he wanted her to have what was his. That got her tearful and she told him she loved him. Leonard held her tighter.

"Don't matter about me," he said. "I aim to take care of you, Maya."

"I don't understand."

"You don't have to. Not right now."

He let her go then and told her to run on to the house to help him fix supper. Maya smiled and wiped her eyes and began to skip childishly, deliriously toward the kitchen.

When he glanced to the eastern sky, above the tree line, Leonard saw a banditry of titmice on the wing, as he listened to the distress call that propelled them.

"Now look here," Prance said. "If you want to burn outside those breaks, a thousand acres will go up faster than whistlin' piss. Not to mention the attention of the local fire brigade."

Lambert sat on the Bronco's tailgate. He looked up from his map, offering Prance marginal status in the business at hand. Lambert had changed clothes, swapping his dress slacks for tactical khakis, along with a long-sleeved camouflage shirt.

"Settle down," he said.

"And if the smoke don't draw him out?"

"Then I'll just burn the goddamn house down," Lambert said.

"You know there're air patrols this time of year. Fire towers. They'll send the cavalry. I can't control that."

"That's why Tony here will call it in first," Lucio said, pointing to his driver. "Just a concerned citizen reporting a brush fire."

"A Rural Defense truck with a twohundredgallon tank could take care of the fire," Lambert said.

"And Leonard will be dead from a stray bullet?" Prance said.

"Hunters zeroing in their scopes can be careless," Lambert said. "Out of practice."

"You're both certifiable," Prance said. He wiped sweat from his mustache and shook his head in disbelief. "And no way you're selling that."

"Not our job to sell it," Lucio said. "It's yours."

Prance couldn't meet his eyes and didn't push it, thinking about his paydays. Cash, booze, girls: they all had him tethered to this moment. Might not be such a big deal after all if Lambert was good at his trade.

Prance got in his car and watched Lucio and Lambert as they hiked into the woods, the bald man behind them carrying two canisters of gasoline.

You either tread water in this life, Prance thought to himself, *or swallow it.*

Now where is that asshole going? Chalmers wondered.

The deputy saw Prance heading westbound on the highway, away from the lake, recognizing the hood of that black Crown Vic winking in the high hot sun and closing fast. Chalmers slowed, expecting Prance to do the same, and raised a hand in greeting. But Prance stared straight ahead, an irritated expression on his face, not even a glance at oncoming traffic.

He watched Prance's car shrink in the rearview mirror. Ever since pulling over a naked and lockjawed William Watkins, Chalmers had been mulling just what had inspired Prance to allow Watkins to walk out of the Trickum County jail. He couldn't chalk it up to laziness. There were plenty of rumors. The sheriff owed Prance one, Chalmers had heard, and when there were layoffs in CID a year ago the fat bastard hadn't even broken a sweat, maintaining his position as chief investigator. Prance's assistant and one crime scene tech handled most of the workload. Prance's drinking and gambling were common knowledge. But Prance showed just enough competence to avoid any department action. He wasn't stupid, Chalmers knew. Just reckless. And dirty as a whorehouse dollar.

Which was why Chalmers turned his patrol car around to follow Prance.

Chalmers hung back, watching as Prance's Crown Vic eventually turned off the highway. Chalmers took note of the secondary road Prance was now on. Chalmers drove another mile, passing the outer woods that surrounded Leonard Moye's property.

Chalmers slowed and turned at a sign partially concealed by wax myrtle. The narrow road led to an unpopular boat landing, a secluded spot in disrepair, known to local anglers as the Panic Pond.

The lot was empty, the landing itself splattered with so much bird shit, Chalmers thought, it looked as if herons had taken up paintball for a hobby. He radioed dispatch with his location, lied when he said he was checking out possible vandalism at the picnic area.

Chalmers grabbed his binoculars from the posse box in the front seat and got out. From habit he glassed the pond, spotted a snakebird spearing its lunch, another swimming with its long slender neck and dagger-shaped beak above the waterline.

He circled the pond and walked in the direction of the firebreak Prance had taken. No sign of him now. He followed a trail into thick pinewoods, listening to the birdsong, squirrels barking overhead, the hollowed thrum of a woodpecker working on a dead tree. Chalmers felt sweat on his forehead. Gnats swarmed around him. He began to wonder if his snooping through the woods was a waste of his time. His reservations grew when he came upon an empty feeder, knocked on its side and showing claw marks from a hungry black bear. He looked up at a nearby tree stand thirty feet off the ground, climbing sticks, a bow hunter's roost. And a reminder he was still on public land. He kept on.

The woods changed, the pines growing more uniform, posted signs tacked to tree trunks indicating he was about to cross onto paper company land. Chalmers spotted a patch of loblollies marked for removal and followed one of the pine rows to a firebreak and heard a motor winding away, back in the direction of the highway. He wondered if it might be the land manager. Or was it Prance?

Chalmers followed the firebreak for a quarter of a mile, left the trail and entered swampier woods, heading in the general direction of Leonard Moye's place. The canopy grew thick enough to obscure the sun and cool the air a few degrees.

He stopped and sniffed.

The odor was mild at first, but distinct. The smell of burning leaves and brush.

Then a few hundred yards ahead of him Chalmers spotted the first lazy column of smoke rising above the tree line.

Lambert left Lucio and his driver at a shallow creek less than a mile from where they had rendezvoused with Prance. He consulted his map, and then looked around, admiring the symmetry of the pine plantation. They were trespassing on a ten-acre rectangle designated "Project No. 128" by the Southland Paper Company, now wholly owned by Lucio, The Mayor, and their friends in Tamaulipas. The tract was surrounded on three sides by firebreaks, marshland forming a natural border to the east

Lambert headed for the flooded timber, the M21 slung over a shoulder. He entered a stand of bald cypress, the roots exposed over soft ground. There was a frying hum of insects in the air. Lambert stopped to glove up and then ascended a ridge that, according to his map, overlooked the southern edge of Leonard's property. The little bit of elevation gave him some perspective, and he looked into a pine flat with a pair of binoculars. He spotted the slick bald head of Lucio's driver, his shirt unbuttoned, empty gas can at his feet. Lucio had already lit the fire.

Staying low, Lambert moved laterally to a nearby windfall and flattened in a comfortable firing position, checking his sight lines and adjusting the rifle. He took a suppressor from the pack around his waist and attached it to the twenty-two-inch barrel, then popped the box magazine into place, pulled back the operating rod, and released the safety.

Lambert tucked in his elbow. Put an eye to the riflescope.

And took a deep breath.

Lucio was about to remind his driver that he had a phone call to make when the 7.62 mm bullet blew through the man's head, Tony's face erupting before his body pitched forward. Lucio wheeled around at the rifle report, flashed a savage smile before diving behind a thickset pine.

They had already started the fire, and flames were spreading quickly. Lucio peered around the tree trunk, looked back toward the ridge. Another round clipped bark inches from his head. He got to his feet, not totally surprised by Lambert's betrayal. He waited a few seconds before sprinting parallel to the burn line, using the smoke as cover. He cleared the fire, juking left, cutting right, vectoring away from what he assumed was Lambert's position on higher ground.

But Lucio's evasive moves couldn't compensate for the kill zone he had unknowingly entered, or the fact Lambert had stayed mobile and moved with him. It happened near the swamp, Lucio beside himself, trying to catch his breath while considering a risky slog through submerged timber to an island a hundred yards away.

The round snapped Lucio's spine in two and he fell parallel to the water's edge, limbs unfeeling and useless. But his mind remained momentarily alert.

He laid there, his head sinking into muck as he gasped for air. Lucio had expected Lambert to finish him off and was disappointed that he had not. He wondered if he would still get to Maya and dispose of the old man.

But what did it really matter now?

Lucio took shallow breaths and stared at the shoreline. Felt insects land and scuttle atop his head. After a time he heard voices. He tried to call out but his own voice failed him. A dragonfly landed on a fingertip and he watched the insect spitefully, wishing he could close his hand and crush it.

Instead Lucio blinked a few times.

He felt nothing.

No pain. No regret, only fleeting impressions of his life. The desire to corrupt simply for the stimulation corruption offered.

He thought about Maya, too. Heavy-lidded, the girl taking a drugged walk around a hotel room, spaghetti strap falling off one shoulder, her neck purple from love bites.

Lucio figured he was hallucinating when he heard her voice, that girlish timbre, telling him it was okay to be afraid.

I fear nothing, he told the hallucination.

You should, it said back.

Not even when black unblinking eyes broke the surface of the swamp water.

Watching. Waiting.

Lucio still felt nothing when the alligator emerged from the reeds, latched on to a leg, and dragged him away from shore.

He felt nothing until the water began to fill his lungs.

Only then he tried to scream.

"I thought you put your fire out?" Maya said.

Leonard had opened a few cans of sardines for his cats. He looked up, squinted, seeing the column of smoke above the woods to the east. *Paper company,* he thought. No reason why they should be doing a burn right now. Their timber was so healthy and well maintained hardly a pine cone was out of place.

The smoke was slanting toward his property.

"What's wrong?"

"Brush fire. May be on my land."

"Is it bad?"

"Could be if it's not knocked down quick," Leonard said.

He considered the risks.

"Don't care for the size of that breeze. I ought take me a look."

Leonard slung the lever-action rifle over his shoulder and grabbed a shovel, thinking he would check for spotting close to his property line, be sure the fire didn't make a jump before somebody could get out there with a water tank.

"What do I do?" Maya said.

"Don't worry. You mind feeding these hungry buggers?"

A catchorus of complaint answered him before Maya could.

"Be careful."

"Keep an eye out," he said. "Any sign of trouble, you take that tunnel past the barn. It'll spit you out near the roads."

"What about the other way?"

Leonard gave her a stern look and shook his head.

"Don't ever go there."

He started off in the direction of the smoke. A flock of blackbirds wheeled through the air. Then came the rifle shot. Followed by another a few minutes later.

By the time he had crossed his field, the fire had intensified to a high blaze. Leonard heard snapping twigs and the *whoosh* of grass going up and quickened his pace into the pine flats.

The smoke grew thicker, still coming at him. Directly ahead a snakespine of flames ate its way across the forest floor.

And there was a body on the ground, close to the burn.

Leonard broke into a run, almost immediately short of breath and unexpectedly panicked. His lower back pained him, but he was determined to get to that body before it set fire. He threw down the shovel, grabbed the dead man by an ankle, and pulled him away from the flames, leaving a swath of blood and brain matter. He turned the body over, cursed at the sight of the disfigured face.

He considered using the spade to put out the flames nearest him when he heard a familiar voice.

"Hold it right there!"

Leonard dropped the man's leg and thought to go for his pistol.

"Do it and I'll shoot."

Leonard's glasses had slipped down his nose. He tipped his head back and looked around, hands away from his body.

Chalmers appeared through the blowing smoke, his gun pointed at Leonard's midsection. Leonard raised his hands.

"I know this ain't lookin' too good," he said, "But I-I—"

"Looks like you shot him and was of a mind to hide him," Chalmers said.

"I saw the smoke, heard shots, and come running. He was dead already. Means there's a gunman loose hereabout, if you want to think about being in the open like this."

"Well, shit," Chalmers said, and looked around nervously.

Leonard made a face and hunched his shoulders. An ache in his stomach almost doubled him over.

"What's wrong?"

"Just a pain, kind of in my chest now. It'll pass. Always does."

Leonard gestured to the body on the ground.

"Jack, you know damn well I'd admit if I shot this man."

Smoke tearing his eyes, Chalmers kept his weapon trained on Leonard, but he was fast losing interest, in his own estimate of what had gone down here.

"Move that body out of the way of the fire."

Leonard complied, wincing noticeably. The trees swayed. Smoke swirled around them.

"Can I pick up my rifle?" he said.

"Shoulder it backward, finger off the trigger. Now tell me who you're hiding at the house, because I know somebody's there."

"Her name is Maya."

"A girl?"

"She's in trouble," Leonard said, looking at the corpse again. "Reckon he's part of it. Can't account for him gettin' shot, but men have come before onto my land, Jack. Tried to kill her."

"What kind of men?"

"They were from, from—"

"Leonard?"

He choked back a cough and clutched at his chest with his free hand before dropping to his knees while the woods crackled around them.

"Well, shit," Chalmers said again.

TEN

MAYA SAT INDIAN-STYLE NEAR THE garden stroking Miss Annie.

She watched the field and the woods beyond it. There was a lot more smoke now in the time Leonard was gone. Maya thought it had been too long, however, and wondered if he was okay. She felt a pang of anxiety, as if sensing he needed help wherever he was.

She picked up the cat and Annie went slack in her grip, trusting her.

Then Annie literally exploded in her hands.

The cat's lower half disappeared in an instant. Maya still clutched the other half as some of the cat's viscera spilled into her lap.

Maya screamed, tasting flecked blood on her lips. She dropped the cat's remains and jerked her head toward the barn as the bird-feeder exploded above her.

She stayed on hands and knees, sobbing as she scrambled to the front door, mostly in shadow and less of a target as another bullet scored the doorjamb in front of her. The door stood open. Maya tumbled inside the house and went crawling down through the trap-door, scared out of her wits.

She threw back the rug and yanked on the latch. Dropped down feet first into the tunnel, banging her elbows and knees, and began to squirm in the dark, in the direction of the caves and away from the rifleman near the barn.

The tunnel was only a little more than three feet in diameter. The passage widened like a drainpipe, the floor crackling with the husks of insects. The chute slanted downward, and after a few minutes of frenzied crawling Maya sensed she was entering a large underground cavern. She hazarded a glance back and saw a beam of light faintly crisscross the darkness.

She muffled a cry and began groping in every direction, for a ceiling, a jut or ledge, the path more uneven as it descended. Maya moved toward the sound of trickling water.

She bumped into rock formations, columns of gypsum determining her course. The footing grew slick as a hard-boiled egg. She reached the edge of a water pool. Something passed over her toes and Maya gasped. From behind her a voice echoed down the tunnel.

"Are you okay?"

"Leonard? Is that you?"

A long pause followed.

"No. It's not."

"Who are you then?"

"I promised His Honor you wouldn't suffer," Lambert called out. "But I lied."

Lambert had unloaded the rifle, pocketed the remaining brass, and left the M21 behind a blackberry bush by the front porch before entering the house. He immediately drew his sidearm and fired. There was an explosion of wood and plaster as Marjean's headless body rocked in her chair. Cats scrambled under the furniture. Lambert looked at the mannequin in amusement and then cleared the rest of the house. Back in the front hallway he studied the hatch-style door in the floorboards and grinned. A handprint told him which direction to go.

Wearing a headlamp he soldiercrawled thirty yards until the man-made tunnel widened, into what he assumed was a natural passage through limestone. He crouched and played the light across the tunnel, noting the umbilical chutes to his right and left, the junction of holes ahead.

A chimney hole above him looked as if it was washed out periodically by rainwater, explaining the deposits of sand and clay around his feet. He could feel a cool draft coming from one of the chutes, and when he passed his light over the floor transparent crickets gleamed like dimes on a sunny city sidewalk.

Lambert understood that the South Georgia countryside was known for its caverns, miles of passages in some areas, the limestone bedrock eroded and hollowed by a hundred million years of seeping water and filled with all manner of speleothem. He was also aware how easily a person could get disoriented in look-alike tunnels. Or be pinned down by a rockfall or step right off a hundred-foot drop and become a permanent addition to the caves.

When he was a boy, an uncle of his from Walker County had told Lambert stories about the Hodag, which was a legend of a caver who had lost his way and never been found. But the Hodag didn't perish. Adapting instead to cave life, one leg grew longer than the other so it could walk upright despite the uneven terrain. *"You'd know the Hodag had gotcha,"* his uncle would tell him, *"When you squirmed through a sand crawl and something pulled off your boot. Or when your markers just disappeared, or your supplies vanished, water bottles got punctured. The mischief of a white-eyed man with a stilted walk, with skin you could see through, and nails mineralized razor-sharp."*

Lambert dropped his voice to an old man's octave, putting on a cracker accent.

"It's Leonard, sweetie. Are you okay?"

Maya knocked her head against a jut. Smarting from the pain, her eyes filled with tears. Sharp-edged rock she crawled over cut her knees and palms. She scrambled from one pillar to another inside the cavern.

It was then Maya remembered the box of matches in the pocket of her jeans.

She needed to put as much distance between her and the chilling voice. Lighting one match after the other, she arrived at the entrance to a sand crawl. Out of options and with no idea of where it led, she lay flat, covered her mouth, and began to sob.

Focus, girl, she told herself.

What would Leonard do?

Lambert took a measured breath and listened, hearing Maya's sobs echo from deeper within the cave complex. The largest of the sand crawls seemed the obvious choice, he thought, and tried to imagine his prey blind and in flight mode, oblivious to her surroundings and forced to feel her way forward.

He stooped, the crawl at one point closing so tight his shirt ripped as he squeezed through the opening. Lambert found himself in a medium-sized room and stood up straight. The ceiling was at least thirty feet high and draped with stone and straw-shaped stalactites and organ pipes. Water dripped from the ceiling, drops falling off the dagger-like tips of rock overhead, or trickling down the cave walls.

In no hurry, Lambert clicked off the headlamp and stood in the darkness for a moment, his heartbeat the only sound in a world that few had known.

He turned on the light and walked to the edge of a subterranean pool. Focused the beam of his light on the water. An albino crayfish no bigger than his middle finger scavenged along the shallow end, a speck of translucent white against the tartar-colored flowstone. Lambert looked back one time and committed the path to memory. Then he raised his chin and sniffed phosphorous from a recently extinguished match head.

Lambert left the pool and crouched at another junction of sand crawls. He cupped a hand around his mouth as if hollering into an old bullhorn and bayed like a hound.

The baying boomed down the chutes and up the chimneys. Bats took wing. A whimper echoed from deep in the caverns. He squirmed through a crawl to his right and howled.

Million years from now they'll find your bones, Maya!

You hear me?

Well, do you, you little whore?

Maya emerged from the crawl, immediately feeling warm air and the expanse of another cavern. She closed her eyes and fought the urge to scream again, breathing erratically, mind reeling from thoughts of the cavern walls closing in, smothering her. Then that guttural voice bayed again, closer than before.

Maya remained in a crouch until she could steady her breathing. A tremor ran through her body. She struck a match, counted ten left in the little red box.

The match light, tiny as it was, provided some comfort. But it didn't last long. Maya's fingertips began to burn, and she waved the match out, and then quickly struck another.

Although Maya couldn't see past a foot or two, she sensed the enormity of the room she found herself in. She heard falling water and came to a wall and put her hand against it. Followed it down by touch and then lit another match. She found herself on a slope, and patted and pawed the stone around her.

Half of the remaining matches lighted her to the edge of a black pool, the tiny nimbus of light winking at its reflection on the water. A blind salamander scuttled away, the amphibian chalk-white, with red feathery gills, its finned tail waving to Maya as it disappeared beneath the surface.

She followed the ripple, and then leaned over. Lit another match and held out her hand, noticing the flame bend in a draft.

Stones, three in all, had been arranged to allow for crossing.

She was down to the last match when Maya found herself on a flowstone beach, staring at a kerosene lamp.

And all kinds of copper contraptions.

Lambert negotiated the last sand crawl as if it were a ladder, the juts of rock providing steps slightly off-plumb. He had been careful to note he was drifting continually to the right during his descent, the cave guiding him, as did the odor of sweat and fear that Maya had left behind.

At one point Lambert had to blade himself to pass between walls of rock. He sucked in his stomach, fearing momentarily that he might get stuck, the rock scraping his sternum like sandpaper. He cursed, then listened for a reaction but heard only the faint trickle of water.

"You in here, Maya? I thought I smelled your stinking snatch!"

He entered a cavern that was at least three times the size of the first room he had encountered. He turned his head and swung the light in a long, slow arc, right to left, glimpsing the beach of flowstone and a long narrow canal. There were sheets of calcite and gypsum chandeliers flowering from the bedrock. Water dripped from a wedge growing out of the ceiling, one of many rows of formations arranged like the teeth of a megalodon, an extinct species of shark that, Lambert guessed, might've swam here tens of millions of years ago when ocean covered the coastal plain.

But despite the geological wonders around him, Lambert's attention was drawn to the long wooden sluice that began in one high corner of the room and canted past a copper still with a hooked snout, down through a large box and out again, then drained into what he realized was a depression separated from the pool by a curtain of rock.

He made his way across the water, playing the light over the still, the empty sacks that had held sugar and cornmeal, cans that had held malt, tins that had been filled with yeast. There was an array of clay jugs. A modest moonshine operation, but Lambert was impressed by the ingenuity on display. Leonard, he assumed, had used a naturally occurring stone furnace to heat the still. He had built the sluice, diverting water from another source into the worm box where steam condensed into spirits.

So how did you get your batches out of here?

For a few minutes hunting Maya was secondary to his fascination with Leonard Moye's underground bootleg operation. Lambert inspected the still, looking up into the dark of the cave's ceiling. *Must be blowholes up there,* he figured, feeling a draft, some air circulation. Nearby a dumbwaiter had been constructed from wood planks. A few near the top were curiously broken, shelves big enough to hold a jug that could then be hoisted along a track through an opening only God and Leonard must have known existed.

Somewhere deep in those woods, Lambert speculated, *he had a winch or pulley rigged. Hauled up his batches a few jugs at a time. Then maybe bring down kindling or supplies while he was at it.*

Raised in the shadow of the Cumberland Plateau, as a young boy Lambert had heard tales of moonshiners, a few who were kin, their stills hidden in the ridges and valleys near the Tennessee state line, the tankers they drove loaded down with illegal alcohol. Eluding the law and revenue men with skills that would impress any contemporary stock car driver.

Lambert could tell that Leonard's still hadn't been operational for some time. He worked loose the copper lid. An inch of blackened crust covered the pot's bottom, remnants of the last slop. The mash was reused five or six times, and a master moonshiner had the touch and acumen of a cordon bleu. Lambert could still detect a sweetness, which explained the cans of malt, and the pleasant, yeasty smell it still yielded.

Another odor caused him to turn quickly, casting his light back across the water and up to the junction of crawls, all of which appeared to spill into the big room—an odor like furniture polish. Stale. A moment later a tapestry of gypsum captured a dozen halos, a sooty, orange flame at the center, the reflections kaleidoscoping. Lambert drew his weapon, looking up at a ledge thirty feet high, where the glass orb in her hands illuminated Maya.

Lambert fired a shot at her.

Maya screamed and disappeared from view. The report was deafening as the bullet pinballed around the cavern and splashed into the pool. Lambert saw only the kerosene lamp Maya had been holding growing larger as it fell and then his world went white with fire.

It had been the most beautiful twilight Maya had ever seen, pink ribbons across the sky, and a few fireflies blinking across the yard. Leonard caught one in his side garden, cupping the little beetle to show Maya they wouldn't bite, coaxing a smile from her when the rear end lit up a gooey-looking yellow. Funny to see them this late, he'd said. And then Leonard had told her of an old superstition he had heard as a boy—about how if a lightning bug entered your home there would be one less person or one more person the next day. Maya had asked him if he had seen a lightning bug in the house before she came running across the field that fateful night but he only snorted a reply. Maya noticed a contemplative gleam in his eyes, though, maybe even a little anger.

"Always been satisfied with my own company," Leonard finally said, holding her with his gaze. "But cats and runaway girls are welcome anytime."

Later as darkness fell, he had shown her how to light the hurricane lamps.

"See here," he said, taking one off a hook by the porch. "This one got a long globe. That's the tank. And this here's the wick." Maya followed his bony finger as he pointed out what was what, then removed the glass chimney and lit the wick. The flame was not all that impressive but when Leonard put the globe back the flame grew stronger, glowing white.

"Now you try," he said. "But be careful—break a lamp and it'll go off like a bomb."

He handed the box of matches to Maya, her hand briefly dwarfed inside his. He had a calloused but gentle touch and Maya felt a wave of emotion, not sure if it was love or devotion.

The warmth inside her now was just like that light in the lamp. A comfort for when the world went black again, because Maya didn't trust the notion she would ever truly escape the world she had left behind.

Once Maya lit the last lamp Leonard went inside to fetch Marjean and they all sat on the porch a while, Leonard in his rocking chair, fingers laced *in his lap until he craved a cigarette, offered one to Maya before lighting his own, both of them listening to the night birds and tree frogs and Maya imagined that the mannequin was even enjoying their company. A chubby cat nicknamed Waffles lay at her feet, bathing stubbornly as if there were just too much fur to account for. Leonard had sassafras roots steeping in a pot on the stove. After a time he asked Maya if she would mind pouring tea. She nudged the cat away and went into the kitchen. Lifted the lid and sniffed the rising steam. The roots had turned a deep red color. Maya dipped the mugs as if they were ladles. She took a sip. The taste reminded her of root beer.*

As she walked back outside a light blinked in the living room. Maya stopped and stared, tea sloshing over the rims of the mugs and onto the floor.

The firefly winked at her again, hovering over the settee as if looking for a place to land.

Maya was thinking of that lightning bug, nerves frayed in darkness as she fumbled for the last match in the box. She dropped to a knee and groped for the kerosene lamp, hands trembling, careful not to knock the lamp over and break the fragile globe as Leonard had warned her. She unscrewed the glass chimney and fingered a half-inch of wick, seeing the lamp in her mind.

She imagined Leonard looking over her shoulder now and saying, *Go ahead, girl. Just like I learned you.*

Maya held her breath and struck the match. It flared and the flame steadied. She lit the wick and carefully set the globe in place, waiting for the flame to grow strong.

She took a look around, hoping to discover a way out of the cavern but found nothing, only another chute too narrow for her to squirm through. The lantern threw light only so far. For a scary moment Maya thought the flame was fading. Shadows wavered on the rock walls. She walked fearfully across the island of flowstone to the other side of the still. Where a frayed rope ladder disappeared into the darkness above her.

If Leonard made it, then it'd be good to use, she thought. *Had to be a reason for its being there.*

Had to.

Maya put a foot on the bottom step. She gave it some weight, noticing the small hook on the underside of each step. The wood groaned but held. The rope knotted around the planks was thick and sturdy in places, fraying in others.

She hooked the lantern's handle in the crook of an elbow and began to slowly climb, the ladder swinging with her weight. She was about twenty-five feet from the floor of the cavern when a rock ledge came into view.

One of the planks broke as she stepped on it, splitting in two. Maya's right leg swung out from under her. She dropped a few feet before she came down on another step, which snapped as well, her body dropping further to the next plank, which thankfully held. She grasped with both hands at the steps above her, where the rope linkage was badly frayed, left foot reaching for purchase on the splintered step below. The rails of the dumbwaiter-like contraption creaked loudly.

Don't look down.

She held her breath.

Then the voice of her pursuer echoed from a sand crawl.

With the lantern hanging from the crook of an elbow, Maya swung to one side of the dumbwaiter, wrapped her legs around the rope, and began to haul herself up, one hand over the other. The ledge was within reach. Close enough so she could simply slide her butt over and sit there casual as she would sit on a porch swing.

By lantern light Maya found herself atop a big and level rock formation that overlooked the entire cavern. There was a crawl behind her, another rock ledge over the opening like a canopy. The hoist made of planks and ropes continued another ten feet higher before turning ninety degrees into a tunnel, like train tracks through a mountainside.

Sweat-soaked and trembling after her climb, Maya looked up at the fluted stone glimmering in the light. But her sense of wonderment was fleeting. The man's voice seemed nearer and more chilling. *You! Down! There! You. Little. Bitch!*

Maya crouched in the crawl canting upward from the ledge, leading with her lantern. But quickly the rock closed around her, abrading her shoulders and back. Not only could she go no further, Maya realized she could be stuck in the crawl.

Nowhere to go, she buried her face in the crook of an arm and cried.

A few moments passed. Maya, unmoving, was turning numb. She focused on her breathing, the lantern light illuminating about six feet of an impassable crawl space. Maya let go of the handle and rested her arms, hoping she had disappeared far enough into the passage that the light wouldn't show from the floor of the cave. She focused on that steady glow. Felt a draft of warm air come down the wormhole.

Moments later Maya heard a rock skitter down the slope of flowstone on the cavern floor. The man was somewhere down there Maya knew, stalking her, and alert for any sound.

Maya let out a deep breath and tried again to wiggle forward. Her tank top snagged against a bulge, the rock digging between her shoulder blades. Something warm spread across her back. *Not even a fox on an empty stomach could've made it*, as Leonard might have said. Maya recalled every inflection, his manner of speech with clarity, his words stored verbatim in her mind.

She could summon any conversation. Play it back word for word.

She closed her eyes and let out a long shuddering sigh.

"Break a lamp, and it'll go off like a bomb ..."

Maya opened her eyes and forced herself to relax. She shifted her hips painfully, then squirmed backward, freeing herself from the straitjacket of rock losing its grip on her body. She was able to crouch again, then stoop, shielding the lantern with her body as she backed up.

She glanced over her shoulder, saw Lambert's flashlight playing around the walls of the cave and the hanging speleothem. She turned slowly and crept to the brink of the ledge, looked down, suddenly dizzy from the height. Lambert stood directly below, back to the flowstone wall, looking over the still.

Maya raised the lantern in both hands. The light took on an added brilliance as she breathed into the chimney's mouth, illuminating nearby stalactites. Lambert looked up, seeing a halo effect, then Maya's face within the halo.

He was quick, firing a shot. The bullet chipped rock above her head.

Maya fell backward, letting go of the lantern. The gunshot echoed.

Followed by the fiery explosion of the lamp and the squeals of a man in agony.

She heard the frantic splashing water below her, followed by screams. Could smell the burning man as clumps of fire smoked on the cave floor. Maya crawled along the ledge, grabbed a rail on the dumb-waiter, and began to climb.

The ladder ended at an opening in the rock wall where a new set of tracks appeared.

The shaft tunneled wide enough to fit a few of those crock jugs she had seen lying around the still. She struggled into the dank shaft, knees and forearms gashed by the crude wooden ties, swallowing dust as the screams behind her stopped.

There were no junctions. The track sloped only one way—up.

After a time a pinhole of daylight appeared.

The pinhole widened with every foot of progress she made until the chimney became flush with light. Maya negotiated moss-covered ledges, scaling them like a seasoned cliff dweller, following Leonard's dumbwaiter to the surface.

A cast-iron winch and a wheelbarrow awaited her.

Maya grabbed handfuls of dirt and sand and leaves for traction and emerged from the mouth of the cave entrance. Outside there was nothing but warm, waning light, the silence afforded by the deep woods.

She looked for the smoke and ran.

ELEVEN

BY THE TIME DEPUTY SUMMERLIN spotted the girl limping along the shoulder of State Route 14, a truck from the Rural Fire Defense had successfully extinguished the brushfire with hoses and hand tools.

He eased his cruiser onto the shoulder, hit the light bar, and got out. He was shocked by the girl's appearance. Maya was filthy, her hair an unbrushed bramble, with a dirt-smudged face and every joint and knuckle skinned raw.

He stopped a few feet from her and smiled. She glowered at him, eyes deep in their sockets.

"You must be Maya," he said.

Maya looked toward the woods as if considering a run for it.

"Where's Leonard?"

"Asking where you are," he said, then gave her an appraising once-over. "You are scratched to hell, girl. Want me to call an ambulance?"

She shook her head.

Summerlin gestured toward his patrol car.

"Now's about the time I try and establish your identity, age, then either take you to Juvenile Services or just give you a ride to Deputy Chalmers and let him deal with you."

He glanced at his watch and shrugged.

"Yeah, I agree—we'll let Chalmers deal with it. I'm due for an end-of-shift and the topwater bite is damn good this time of night anyhow."

Maya let the deputy guide her into the passenger seat of the patrol car. Exhaustion set in, and for a moment Maya thought she might vomit. She closed her eyes as Summerlin merged onto the highway.

When she opened her eyes walls of pine were whipping by and in the distance a few wisps of smoke lingered above the tree line.

"I'm no juvenile," Maya said, her voice laced with rage. "And you never told me where Leonard is."

Summerlin shot her a look, curious about how a routine day on the job could end like this.

"He's back at the house. With Chalmers and the Doc."

"Doc?"

"Heart problems be my guess," he said.

Maya covered her eyes and began softly to cry. Summerlin said nothing. He turned down one of the firebreaks.

They passed a trailhead on the way to Leonard's where an ambulance and three county vehicles were parked. Ronnie Prance was one of a small group that included a fire ranger, the medical examiner, her assistant investigator, and a land manager who had been summoned from the banks of the river and was still wearing a pair of chest waders. Prance watched Summerlin's Crown Vic and its passenger with clear interest.

Summerlin raised a hand to the driver of a passing pickup that carried a large water tank in the bed. Then at the next intersection he hung a left onto a dirt road with a canopy of long arching oak boughs.

After twenty minutes they crossed the plank bridge and drove the long, winding one-track road onto Leonard's property. Maya's mood lifted as they passed the field of scarecrows that looked ominous as the light disappeared around them.

Several police cars, a Fire & Rescue truck, and a station wagon were parked in front of Leonard's house. The side garden and yard had been isolated with yellow crime scene tape.

Summerlin sighed and said, "The bass of Lake Seminole will live to swim another day."

He put a hand on Maya's shoulder before she could open the door.

"What do you want?"

"I'm not a fan of mysteries," he said. "But there's a dead man and what looks like arson. Bullet holes in that house the size of Oreo cookies. Make no mistake we need straight talk from y'all. Understand?"

Maya stared at the hand on her shoulder until Summerlin removed it.

Then she got out of the cruiser and ran toward the house.

Chalmers heard the kitchen door slap shut and stepped into the hallway, hand on the butt of his service pistol, thinking Maya appeared to have escaped a premature burial.

"I need to ask you some questions."

But she pushed past the deputy and entered the bedroom.

"Leonard? Leonard?"

A large man with a stethoscope turned and regarded her curiously. Maya had never seen a doctor dressed like he was. He wore a white cowboy hat, boots, and denim jeans. A patchwork of colors extended the length of each sleeve on his matching chambray shirt.

Behind him Leonard lay on the iron bedstead, a sheet folded back at his waist, his face pale as glacier ice.

"Are you okay?"

Leonard squinted at her and smiled.

"You look like dog snot," he said in a raspy voice. He took a sip of water from a bedside glass.

Chalmers followed her into the room and cleared his throat.

She looked at him.

"What the hell happened to you?"

"I got lost," she said. "Should've known better than to go exploring the caves on my own."

When she faced Leonard again she saw a glimmer of approval in his eyes.

Chalmers crossed his arms and stood in the doorway as if he didn't believe a word she said. The doctor took a bottle of peroxide and some cotton swabs from his medicine bag when Maya shook her head stubbornly.

"Who are you?" she said.

"This here's Doctor Agnew," Leonard said. "Only man I'd let stick me with a needle."

"What happened?"

"Likely it's *angina*," Agnew said. "Could be a mild heart attack. Get him to the hospital, we'll know more, but—"

"Ain't going," Leonard said.

Agnew rolled his eyes.

"Most I can do for him here is aspirin and nitroglycerin pills. You're a fit man for your age, Leonard, but it's time to give up the tobacco and fried squirrel."

Leonard took a few painful breaths and fell back against the pillows. He let Agnew take his pulse, then listen to his chest again with the stethoscope.

It became obvious to Maya that Leonard not only tolerated the doctor, but also liked him.

"I thought you told me you didn't have any friends?" Maya said.

The big doctor smiled.

"Funny," he said, turning to Leonard. "How some misanthropes have the most loyal acquaintances."

"Friends are overrated."

"And family?"

"No use for that either."

Agnew looked over at Chalmers and smiled.

"You know, Leonard. If it wasn't for Jack here, you'd be pissing on the pearly gates about now."

"Ought to get him arrested for kissing me."

Chalmers took a step toward the bed.

"Okay, so I overreacted? But it's called *mouth-to-mouth*, you ungrateful crackpot."

"You sweet on me, aren't you?" Leonard said slyly.

All the humor had gone out of Chalmers's eyes, however. He motioned for Agnew.

"Can you tend to her in the kitchen? I need a word with Leonard in private."

"I'm staying," Maya said.

"You go on, Miss Maya," Leonard said.

"He's right," Agnew said. "Let's get you cleaned up."

But before going with the doctor she looked back at Leonard. He said all he could with his eyes, and then she was gone.

Chalmers closed the door, adjusted the bedside lamp, then pulled over a chair and turned it backward so that he faced Leonard. Leonard sighed and blinked his cloudy eyes.

"So I saw you at the pharmacy, right?" Chalmers said. "Ronelle told me you'd been by to make some unusual purchases."

"You should've said hello. Been so long."

"For a while I assumed you were dead," Chalmers said. "Then I moved back to Trickum last year and heard some stories about the crazy old man with the mannequin."

"You act like you don't got a clue where I live. And what's this business pretending we aren't kin? You do got some talent for treating me like a stranger."

"You are a stranger. And I'd say it's a talent that runs in the family. We're like one big poster child for estrangement."

A mutual resignation quieted both men. Leonard seemed to have trouble making Chalmers out against the lamp.

"Maybe it's time—time we make peace with what happened?"

"No way," Chalmers said. "I can never forgive them."

Leonard nodded and looked out the window.

"You got a family of your own?"

"I do. They're happy enough knowing that you don't exist."

"Well—that's nice."

"Well?" Chalmers said, mocking him. "Some families go to hell so fast they're not worth the regrets. To think my daddy run off with his brother's wife and abandoned a baby? Who could do such a thing? And I come to find out later that my mother, she was barely a day in the ground, dead from the big C. I took her name and made damn sure I never acted like the no-account son of a bitch he was."

"Despite what he done to your mother—and me—your daddy loves you."

"What he did to my mama, and you, and to all of us begs to differ. I wouldn't piss on him if he was on fire."

A heavy silence fell over the bedroom. Chalmers studied the chifforobe as if some childhood memory had emerged and done a derisive little dance for him.

"So do you know anything about Percy? How is my brother?" Leonard said.

"He's doing poorly, last I heard. Housebound and bedridden."

Leonard frowned, then a deeper sadness became apparent in his eyes. Chalmers looked away. He knew what was coming.

"And Marjean—how she be?"

Chalmers lowered his head. Took to pulling at the hair around a tattoo on his forearm, a nervous habit he'd had since childhood that had only worsened with age.

"Frail. Worn out, I hear. Got a half brother lives over in Colquitt, but we don't talk. None of us talk. When I got back from Kuwait and left the service Daddy tried to mend fences with me, but I wasn't having it. Told him to go to hell."

"Your daddy and me are going to the grave with an awful lot of hate in our hearts."

"Don't I know it?"

Leonard's mood darkened.

"If that's all the news you got, I'll kindly ask you to leave my house now."

Chalmers didn't budge. He stared a hole through the wall and then turned his angry gaze on his uncle.

"I knew something was off when I came out here the first time. Just what in the hell are you mixed up in?"

"Nothing. There's nothing going on I can't handle."

"Who the hell is this girl you've taken up with?"

"Just a friend. Otherwise, none of your business."

"My business should be to jail you right now for murder and God knows what other felonies you've committed where that girl is concerned."

"Now you wait just a minute. I never laid a hand on her. She just had no place to go is what I'm telling you."

"So that body in the woods?" Chalmers said, and then raised his right hand to count finger by finger. "That military-issue M21 we found by the front door, the beat-up hatch in the floorboards, crawl spaces that go underground, the house shot to shit?"

Chalmers kept his five accusatory fingers upraised for effect. "So?"

"And a young girl with no ID? City kid by her attitude. Where'd you get her?"

Leonard waved him off.

"She just wandered by is all. Now get out of here."

Chalmers drew a calming breath.

"Yeah, if that's how you want it, you stubborn bastard. But there is going to be an investigation here. I don't mean a half-ass Ronnie Prance job. After I write my report, that girl, Maya, is coming with me. Or the GBI will get a phone call. If they haven't already."

Leonard made an effort to sit up.

"No, Jack," he said. "She's safe here. And she don't want any more attention than she's already had."

"So all this business, it's about her?"

Leonard looked into his nephew's eyes, anxiety apparent on his face.

"She's got no family."

"That makes two of you," Chalmers said cynically.

"No home. She has seen things would make your skin crawl. And things been done to her that no child should ever have to suffer."

"That's it, I'm calling the feds."

"There's no police department can protect her, you hear me? I know you can make that paperwork look prettier than what appears to be."

"Excuse me?"

Leonard paused before grimly expressing what scared him most.

"That girl will die once you take her off my place. There are some powerful people after her. They're dug in deep, and up to something down here. Buying up all the land. Can't even trust the cops, Maya told me."

"Even me?"

Leonard looked down.

"You're the only one I trust, Jack."

Chalmers could barely hide his astonishment. He looked at the bedroom door, then again at Leonard. When he spoke his voice was low and steady.

"I heard how you made your money," he said. "Heard the crazy stories, about how *yours* was the last face some men ever saw. But I always judged you to be a fair man according to your code. Daddy wasn't sorry for what he did, and neither is Marjean. But it makes me sick to my stomach. That pain will never dull."

"Listen here," Leonard said.

But Chalmers talked over his uncle, his voice rising.

"Now I don't blame you for who you are and the life you've chosen for yourself. You can scoot around in that Studebaker, scare the bejesus out of children with your evil eye, and play house with a damn mannequin. But you can't, I mean will not, take in runaways like a neighbor's cow wandered off the pasture."

"Keep your voice down."

"I don't care who hears me. It had to be said."

Leonard's commitment to Maya was still plain as the worry lines of his forehead.

"I'm putting it to you," he said to Chalmers. "As blood kin. Look around at what's happened here and help me. For Maya's sake, let it lie. I'm warning you."

When Chalmers walked into the kitchen, he found Agnew and Summerlin sitting around the table, watching Maya idly leafing through the pages of a small book. But she was more tense than hostile to their presence.

She had changed tank tops. Bandages covered her raw elbows, shins, and knees. But her skin was cleaner, face washed, hair brushed. Chalmers saw for himself that beneath the layer of dirt and grime a very beautiful young woman had been hiding.

Chalmers stared at the branding scar on Maya's shoulder. It renewed his anger, but with a different focus. He reached past her and lifted the cover of the book to see what she was reading. It was a leather-bound edition of a pocket medical reference. Chalmers looked at Agnew.

"Yours?"

"Seems Maya has a talent," Agnew said.

"Talent?"

Summerlin looked at his watch and said, "Time."

Maya closed the book.

"*The cue-cue-tane-ee-us and sometimes systemic reactions,*" she said. "*Associated with vaccinations for smallpox . . . a generalized condition of widespread lesions resulting from sensitivity response to smallpox vaccinations . . .*"

"She even knows what those words mean?" Chalmers said.

Maya looked at him.

"Not all of them. Got Leonard's Bible near memorized."

"But you can see the words in your mind, right?" Agnew said.

"Like I'm looking at a blackboard," she said.

"Now do the numbers from the table."

Maya spouted off a sequence of numbers.

Chalmers shrugged.

"So she's got a good memory."

"Not just a good memory. A photographic memory," Agnew said. "She can scan a page or hear someone talking, and the words get stored forever."

He pointed a finger at Maya's temple.

"Up here," Agnew said.

Maya smiled as if it were no big deal.

"Forever?" Chalmers said.

"Whatever I want or need to remember."

Chalmers wanted to ask Maya a few more questions, but he turned his head as a convoy of vehicles, led by Ronnie Prance's unmarked cruiser, appeared on the long road to Leonard's house. Chalmers nodded to Summerlin. They put on their campaign hats and walked outside.

Agnew leaned close to Maya, as if to deliver a message in confidence.

"You keep those cuts clean. And tell Leonard to take his nitro pills or my next visit will be to shoo the buzzards away from his bed. Understand?"

"Is he going to be okay?"

"Reckon it'll take more than heart failure to kill Leonard Moye."

"How long have you been friends with him?" she said, trying not to look out the window. She began to tremble.

"Long time. Long enough to know there aren't many like us."

"Who's *us*?"

Agnew mulled her question.

"Just those folks that, uh, understand a fella like Leonard."

"I understand him," Maya said.

"Yes. I suspect that you do."

"Does this mean I get to stay?"

"Not up to me, dear."

She shot him an anxious look.

"But you can trust Chalmers. My word on that. He's a good man."

"Okay."

Agnew gathered his things, looked up to see Ronnie Prance through the kitchen window, struggling from behind the wheel of his Crown Vic.

"One more thing, Maya."

"Yeah?"

"You and Leonard need to get your story straight right quick."

Prance's assistant, Lorraine Knox, was bagging Lambert's rifle as her boss studied the bullet holes around the doorjamb. Ants and flies swarmed the body of the cat in the yard. Summerlin pondered the camera in his hands, a job the deputy accepted as an imposition.

"Isn't this her job?" he said, gesturing to Knox as she dusted the doorknob for prints. She looked at him and continued dusting.

Prance was oozing sweat and had no use for complaints. It was dark and hot and he still had a red Bronco out in the woods that needed to be disposed of. He stared at the crumpled rug by the hatch in the floor. Had to be a crawl space underneath, but he wasn't going down there. He was irked that Leonard's home was so dimly lit by lamplight.

"Where the hell does that go?" Summerlin said.

"Who knows? Probably where he buries his bodies."

"I once heard Leonard stumbled on a chest of gold stolen by Creek Indians. That's how he came to his little fortune."

Prance shook his head.

"I know exactly how he made his money. Make sure you get photos of all this."

There was a cord-hung lamp with a pull chain over Prance's head, a stained-glass shade. Prance pulled the chain and light spread into the living room. He saw Maya there, sweeping pieces of the mannequin's head into a dustpan. Chalmers stood nearby, watching. Prance was acutely aware that his appearance had ended a conversation.

"What the hell is she doing?" he said.

"Cleaning up the mess," Chalmers said. "A home invader unloaded on Marjean's head."

Prance appraised the scene, his shifty eyes pausing to admire Maya's backside.

"You ever thought that could be evidence?"

"Not until now," Chalmers said with a hint of sarcasm.

"Where is he?"

"Who?"

"Jimmy Carter. No—Leonard. Who the fuck else?"

"He's in the bedroom resting. A-fib is acting up."

"You get statements, hotshot?"

"Yeah."

Chalmers pulled his notebook from a breast pocket.

"The guest of the homeowner, female, eighteen years old, name of *Whitney Womack*, was not present at the time of the shooting. Miss Womack stated she had been lost in the woods south of Leonard Moye's property, and had become disoriented. She did not hear gunshots, nor did she see who started the fire."

Prance cut him off, shaking his head so violently his jowls flapped.

"*Whitney Womack?* Horseshit."

He looked Maya over again.

"Quit that goddamn sweeping, girl. What business you got with Leonard? You ain't no kin to him."

Chalmers looked at Maya, who said, "Leonard is a friend of my uncle, mister. He's kindly watching after me for a few days."

"Oh, yeah?" Prance said, smirking.

Maya nodded humbly.

"Yes, sir."

"And how'd you get all cut up there, girl?" Prance said.

Maya blinked a few times as if confused.

"I mean the scratches and cuts," Prance said. "Like somebody did you some rough loving?"

"I tripped and fell in some thorny bushes."

Prance ran a tongue across his front teeth. Chalmers noted something more than inquisitiveness in Prance's eyes.

"Well, you got to be more careful out there in the woods," Prance said, and then looked at Chalmers.

"Where is he again?'

"Down the hall. First door on the left," Chalmers said.

Prance tugged at his beltline and looked at Maya.

"Don't go nowhere. I ain't through with you."

Ten minutes later Prance reappeared and crooked a finger at Maya in the living room.

"You come with me." To Chalmers he said, "Stay put."

She looked to Chalmers, who held his tongue and nodded. Prance had a sugar sack in his right hand, filled with what appeared to be a quart jar. Chalmers felt a surge of anger.

Prance led Maya through the kitchen and out into the yard. He opened the passenger door of his Crown Vic, having her wait while he cleared out fast food wrappers and empty soda cans. There were camera flashes by the front door as Summerlin snapped photos. Knox was digging for spent cartridges. Maya hoped one of them would turn and notice her but they walked around to the far side of the house.

"Get in," Prance said.

He settled into the seat next to her. He flipped to a clean page in his notebook, clicked a pen, and began doodling.

"So let's cut the bullshit," he said. "I know exactly who you are. Lucio asked me to bring you home."

"Is he here?"

"I don't know where Lucio went. He's vanished. But orders is orders."

Maya stiffened but didn't seem surprised.

"Leonard signed his statement and gifted me a pint of his select stock, right after feeding me that story he concocted. Kind of like the nasty business about a crazy hunter shooting at the house."

Maya felt Prance's eyes on her. Heard him breathing heavily through his mouth. She made fists in her lap. So many times it had begun like this. The breathing, the building lust and contempt.

"What's a matter?" he said. "Cat got your tongue? So you wouldn't know nothing about that, would you—*Maya?*"

She reached for the door handle, but Prance grabbed her wrist and twisted. At her hiss of pain he eased up and looked around to see if anybody was watching.

Maya wiped her eyes, angry with herself for crying.

"What do you want then?"

He felt her tremble and smiled.

"I'm of a mind to haul Leonard in, see how he fares at the county jail for a few days."

"Don't do that. Please."

"Well then, now you do the talking."

"So you know who I am?"

Prance nodded.

"I know most of the men in your life seem to meet an untimely fate as soon as they set foot in Trickum County. You don't know where Lucio is?"

"No."

"Something happened to him, but why should I care? I've got you. And *you* is what *they* are after. How many men you been with? A hundred? Five hundred? Lucio just about worked you to death, didn't he?"

When Maya didn't answer, Prance tilted the notepad so that she could see. He had cartoonishly sketched a woman on all fours, nude, barking like a dog, her rear end dripping semen. Dark thoughts began to cloud Maya's mind.

"So what you want from me?" she said.

"I'm taking you back to Atlanta."

"No, no, you can't do that."

"Then how about a deal?"

"What kind of deal?"

"Reckon you still got some juice in you. I can do a lot for you in return, depending on how you want to play."

"And what about Leonard?"

"What about him? For starters I could charge him with producing liquor without a license. Call the ATF and make a big to-do about it. Those boys from ol' Mexico get through with him, you could probably haul away what was left in a duffel bag."

"Or?"

"I whitewash this mess. And maybe we work out a little exit strategy—together."

"What's it going to cost?"

"Some of that sweetness between your legs to start. You give me that I can do a lot for you in return."

Maya's expression hardened.

"Like leaving Leonard out of this? I don't want trouble for him."

Prance smiled.

"I can make it all go away," he said magnanimously.

Maya turned and looked him straight in the eye.

"Your place or mine?"

Prance let out a nervous-sounding laugh. Then told Maya to wait in the car.

She watched as he waved Knox, Summerlin, and the other deputies over. Prance gestured toward his Crown Vic, apparently explaining something. Chalmers came outside. To Maya he looked worried, his eyes on Prance. Then he looked at her.

Maya shook her head at Chalmers.

Seconds later Prance heaved his bulk behind the wheel again without a glance at Maya. He put the car in gear and drove away, heading for the highway.

"You let her just leave with him?"

Leonard was outside in the yard, shirt unbuttoned, pants undone, looking distraught.

"Prance said she volunteered to give a statement and waived her right to an attorney. Agreed to an interview. He was taking her to the office."

"And you let him?"

Chalmers shook his head.

"Telling Captain Prance what he can and can't do doesn't fall under my job description," he said.

"Something wicked is going on. What are you going to do about this?"

"What needs doing?"

"If you don't, I'll get her back myself."

Chalmers was already walking to his patrol car when Leonard's promise, or threat, stopped him.

He had been the last one to leave. The only sounds were warblers on the pitch, cats crying for their dinner, and the tacking of caddis-flies against the kerosene lamps on the porch.

Chalmers turned and pointed a finger at his uncle.

"Don't be a problem to me, old man."

"The girl is in danger," Leonard said. "And you're too stupid to see it."

"Danger from who?"

Leonard grit his teeth and winced. After catching his breath, he told Chalmers everything he knew or suspected.

When he finished talking Chalmers's face was a study in dismay.

"And she told this to some undercover cop?"

"Who got himself killed," Leonard said. "And she's next."

"It's one hell of a conspiracy," he said. "All the way to City Hall."

Leonard nodded.

"The man plans to run for governor, she says. But he's in deep with this Lucio and the cartel. They're behind the shell companies already bought thousands of acres. Maya told me they're going to build underground labs to cook the drugs and use the river to get them to their distributors. You heard about all those land deals lately, right?"

"I have," Chalmers said. "And you believe Maya?"

"For damn sure. They have every intention of burying her out here. Maya told me she probably wasn't the first person to get the same treatment. They got their hooks in deep. Said this Lucio has had bodies dumped down here already."

"My God. You're implying county law enforcement has been looking the other way."

"Look around you," Leonard said with a flourish of his hand. "Who suddenly owns it all but what I got here? Now I might prefer the company of felines and a mannequin, but I'm no dummy."

"This is outside my pay grade."

"Then call the Feds. Maya has everything he ever told her stowed in that brain of hers. She knows the scheme inside and out. The man confided in her like a wife. He was a fool for her. It's not even about the money or drugs. These bastards want the power that chaos brings. Pretty much his exact words."

"But who's going to believe her?"

"What do you mean?"

"The word of a prostitute," Chalmers said. "Who manipulated a mentally unstable man with wild tales. Exchanged sexual favors for food and shelter."

"You questioning my sincerity?"

"No. But I am a skeptic. It's just too outrageous."

He shook his head and walked away. Was opening the door of his cruiser when the memory of that traffic stop not too long ago hit him.

William Watkins.

He looked back at Leonard.

"You say you whooped up on those men real bad, right?"

"I did," Leonard said. "Dragged one through a briar patch 'fore he got away."

"There were two of them?" Chalmers said.

Leonard hesitated.

"Two, maybe three. It was dark."

Chalmers nodded and got into his cruiser. He cranked the engine, and then put down the window.

"Where are you going?" Leonard said. "Are you going to bring her back?"

"I've got some serious mulling to do. I recommend you get your rest, Uncle Leonard. Don't look so good. Not as spry as you once was."

"Never thought I'd see you all grown up, or ever hear you call me that."

"Likely won't ever hear it again."

"So where do we stand?"

"Something stinks. I'll give you that. I've got a friend at GBI I'm going to call."

Leonard licked a hand and smoothed back his hair, tucked in his shirt. Buttoned his pants. He watched Chalmers drive away.

Alone on his land again, as he had been for many years.

He felt a flutter in his chest, a dull pain that came and went.

Leonard walked back to his house, head down, filled with silent guilt and confusion of purpose. He was scared for Maya.

And, for the first time in his long life, scared for himself.

Chalmers parked in the driveway behind his boat trailer.

His split-level home was located in a development ten miles north of town, the entrance adorned with balloons and heavy signage, headshots of toothy realtors, arrows desperately pointing the way. Only six of the forty lots had been sold when Chalmers and his family had moved to Trickum the previous year.

Ronelle was smoking a cigarette on the porch, her posture a slouch that didn't look too friendly. Chalmers saw her wipe her eyes. He took his time getting out of his cruiser and lingered near the trailer, where his seventeen-foot bass boat was under a blue travel cover.

Normally at that hour, looking at a full twenty-four hours off duty, Chalmers would be getting ready for bed. Early to rise, then easing into the lake before sunup.

But right now he wasn't thinking about fishing.

Ronelle stubbed her cigarette out and stuck the butt inside a pickle jar. She twisted the lid shut and placed the jar behind a rocking chair. When the porch door slapped shut Chalmers took that as his cue to go inside.

He found Cale sitting at the dining room table, tinkering with a radio-controlled car. Chalmers gave him a soft punch in the arm.

"You do those decals yourself? Looks just like the Intimidator's."

"Sure did," Cale said, looking up with a satisfied smile. "Mama said to ask you about taking us to Talladega."

"Oh, really?"

Cale nodded. The boy had grit under his nails. Jeans muddied around the knees. A mop of hair that needed a trim. He loved messing around with go-karts, a gearhead just like Leonard. *Must run in the family*, Chalmers thought. Looking at his son, he felt a nagging uneasiness about Maya. If what Leonard had said was even partly true she had missed everything worthwhile to a normal young girl. Loving parents, food, shelter, school, friends, hobbies, and play. Chalmers hoped the only violence in Cale's adolescence would be confined to books and movies and the spectacle of a frontstretch pileup at the local racetrack.

Chalmers had taken a few moments to think about what Ronnie Prance was up to when his wife spoke behind him.

"Give it here, Jack."

Kelly Anne smiled but had her hand out, gesturing to his duty belt.

Chalmers removed his belt and gave it to her, watched as his wife hung the belt in a hall closet. He followed her into the kitchen. She'd warmed a plate and set it on the counter, macaroni and cheese, a scoop of dressing with a pan-fried pork chop. Chalmers kissed her and sat down. Began moving his food around as if arranging the pieces of a board game.

"So you know who did it?" Kelly Anne said. He had called her earlier about a shooting in the woods, nothing more.

Chalmers shook his head.

They heard heavy footsteps outside the kitchen. A bathroom door slammed shut.

"What's with your little sister?"

Kelly Anne rolled her eyes. She stirred a spoonful of sweetener into a glass of tea and took a sip.

"She's having guy troubles."

"Again?"

"First I heard of this one. Dropped her like a hot brick. Apparently he had an epiphany, found religion, and moved to Florida."

Chalmers rolled his neck and sighed.

"What's going on with you?"

"Why?"

"You're not eating and you brought the job home with you and I thought we had an agreement about that."

Chalmers shrugged and said, "I'm fine."

"Come on, Jack. Don't make me drag it out of you."

Chalmers pushed the plate away and began plucking at the hairs on his forearm. Kelly Anne waited.

"I never told you why my father ran off, did I?"

She sat down on the stool next to him. Placed a hand on his to stop him from worrying all the hair off his arm.

"Jack, what is it?"

"It's hard to talk about," he said.

"I know you were just a baby when it happened."

"That's right. Did you ever hear things?" Chalmers said. "About the Moyes?"

"I'm from Brinson. We didn't talk about people from Trickum. You're all crazy to us."

She smiled at him.

"That's the truth," he said.

Chalmers took a deep breath and got on with it.

"Uncle Leonard still lives out this way, alone, save for with a lot of cats and a mannequin. Well, he lived with a mannequin until today. Somebody blew the thing's head away with a forty-five."

Kelly Anne's head did a little melodramatic dip. Her eyes flickered with the possibility of intrigue.

"Sweet Jesus."

"Yeah." A corner of Chalmer's mouth twitched. "And he is mixed up with a runaway girl."

His wife whistled softly, thinking that over.

"And?"

"My estranged uncle has been protecting her from some criminals. But the girl is with Captain Prance after an incident this evening. Ever since I joined the department you know what I've thought about Prance. And I think he's a big part of the problem."

"He's dirty?"

"Something stinks—bad."

Kelly Anne took her time processing what he had said and hadn't said.

"Prance's covering for somebody, the girl is in more danger, and you want to go get her?"

"Yeah."

"But if you're wrong, there goes your job."

"I'll have the satisfaction of knocking his goddamn teeth out," Chalmers said.

Kelly Anne rested her head on his shoulder.

"Well, I heard the paper mill is hiring."

"I need to know."

Kelly Anne got up and opened the closet where his duty belt hung.

"Be careful," she said. "Don't get hurt. And you be sure to invite your uncle and this girl over for dinner when it's all over."

"My ex-wife got the house, but it'll do for now."

Maya looked around the living room while Prance fetched drinks from the kitchen. The trailer was dingy, furnished with a recliner and television set. A standing ashtray overflowed with cigarette butts. There were no pictures of family, only a few framed photographs of Prance on the lake hoisting trophy-sized bass. She noticed an ant trail disappearing through a cracked window. On the carpeted floor a stain began at one end of the living room and ended at the folding door to the bathroom.

Chalmers parked out of sight at a nearby boat launch, thinking about his call to the deputy on desk duty to confirm Prance had radioed in his end of shift.

He moved quickly through a stand of cypress, and then past an undergrowth of saw palmettos with teeth sharp enough to slice the skin had he been wearing anything other than his khaki uniform pants. He glanced at some Spanish moss overheard, stirring in the breeze, and thought how it would have come in handy earlier that afternoon. *Graybeard* his granddad on his mother's side had called it,

once advising Chalmers that if he ever were trapped in a forest fire
to gather up as much of the plant as he could. The moss sucked up all
the moisture in the air and could slow an approaching line of flames.

The moss also was home to Seminole bats in the summer months,
clumps of bug-filled fur he would rather not touch. He heard the
honk of an egret and Chalmers looked out across the lake. A thick
layer of hydrilla floated on the surface nearby, shimmering in moonlight. Prance's place was fifty yards away.

He had closed the distance to the trailer when a light came on
in the bedroom, followed by the flicker of a television screen. He
heard voices. Chalmers crouched and waited, watching Prance draw
the window blinds. His unmarked cruiser was parked under a prefab
carport.

Chalmers looked at his watch and said *Fuck it* before he made
his way around the trailer to the front door.

When Maya failed to respond to Prance's groping, he pulled his
revolver and held the muzzle inches from her face.

"I know you're dirty, baby girl," he said. "Now get in the shower."

Hearing Lucio's term of endearment triggered a retreat in Maya,
to that place in her mind that could withstand almost any insult,
emotionally and physically. She backed into the bathroom. Prance
followed her, pants zipper down, pistol in one hand, a prescription
bottle in the other.

"Go on," he said.

Maya undressed slowly, her eyes going from the gun to Prance,
knowing that her full attention was required. He twisted the top off
the prescription bottle, fingered a pill out, popped it in his mouth,
and dry swallowed.

"What are those?" she said.

Prance snorted.

"Little something to get my blood up."

Maya parted the curtain and stepped into the shower enclosure, the floor slick with mildew.

"Leave it open so I can watch you," he said.

Prance sat down on the toilet. Leaned over and turned the knobs. The pipes moaned. Then a stream of cold water hit Maya. She yelped, hugging herself, her skin breaking out in chill bumps. Prance laughed. He set the gun next to the sink and slapped Maya on the butt. Then he grabbed an arm and twisted it behind her back.

"Let me see it, girl. I know you ain't shy."

The water began to warm and Maya turned, giving Prance her backside, Prance shifting to the edge of the toilet and for a moment Maya thought the whole throne would shatter under his weight. He steadied himself, then leaned over and put a hand on her rump and let it slide to the inside of her thighs.

Prance pulled his dick out of his pants and began working it to an erection.

"Get you some of that soap," he said.

Maya took the bar of soap from a dish and began lathering her body with circular motions.

She heard Prance climax and glanced at the gun again.

When he caught his breath, Prance opened his eyes and grinned.

"I like to get that first one out of the way," he said, wiping his fingers on a wad of toilet paper. "There's more where that come from."

Prance got up and cut the water off. Handed her a towel. He backed out to give her room to dry off. The revolver was back in his right hand.

A few moments later Prance pulled her out of the bathroom and forced her down the hall.

The bedroom was heavy with the odor of unwashed sheets. Clothes were piled on the floor. Maya inched toward the bed. On the nightstand she noticed a fifth of Early Times, a bottle of antacids, another ashtray brimming with butts. There was a framed movie poster on the opposite wall, a stagecoach and horses, two rustlers in the foreground, with bandanas tied around their necks, a western film that predated Maya by forty years.

Prance turned on the television and fussed with a remote. The passionate grunts of a porno film filled the room, accompanied by bass-heavy funk music that added nothing to the loveless sex on display.

Noting the hand in which he held the pistol, Maya squared off to him and waited expectantly, her eyes flicking from the film poster behind him to Prance while he undressed.

It took some effort but Prance finally got naked, completely at ease with his sagging body. He was obviously proud of the package between his legs. She crooked a finger at him.

"Why don't you put that gun away—*cowboy?*"

He flipped a condom at Maya and with his free hand began trying to get his cock to stand alone.

"Why don't *you* put that on," he said, approaching the bed. "With your mouth."

Maya took the wrapper between her fingertips and flipped it over her shoulder as though she had no use for it.

"I got another idea."

"Oh, really? What's that?"

"Come here," she said.

He inched closer, cautious, jerking his hand away when she reached for the barrel of the revolver.

"I don't think so, darlin'."

"Come on, cowboy. I'm not going to hurt you."

Finger on the trigger, Prance hesitated but decocked the hammer and grinned as she drew the muzzle toward her lips and kissed the crown.

"Oh, girl," he said. "Oh—my God."

She licked the front sight.

"You like that?"

Maya paused to wink at Prance and took more of the muzzle in her mouth. His eyelids fluttered as he watched her go to work on the barrel.

"Yeah, I do," he said. "I like that a lot."

Maya showed some tongue against the blued steel of the revolver. Placed her hand on his chest and slid it down slowly across his belly. She heard him moan with delight and when he tilted his head back she opened one eye, for a peek at Prance's weakening grip.

Chalmers heard a scream and busted into the trailer. He had kicked in the front door and rushed down the hallway before Prance in his erotic daze could react.

It was hard to tell who looked more surprised.

Ronnie Prance, hands in the air, his penis seemingly conjoined to the business end of a .38 Smith & Wesson.

Or Maya, holding the pistol with two hands and determined to use it.

"No, Maya. Don't do it," Chalmers said and made a move.

"Wait now—hold on—she'll blow off my pecker."

When Prance turned his head, Chalmers knocked him down with a straight right hand. Blood sprayed from Prance's ruined nose. Then he swatted Maya's arm away just as she fired, but Chalmers deflected her aim and the bullet hit the roof of the trailer.

Chalmers shook his head, stunned by the concussion. He glanced at the porn showing on the television and yanked out the plug. Then he picked up the revolver, emptied the cylinder, and then snapped his fingers at Maya.

"Get dressed," he said.

She was breathing heavy and watching Prance as he groped on the floor trying to get a hand on Chalmers's leg. Chalmers stepped back and kicked Prance in the head, then reached down and rolled him onto his stomach so he wouldn't strangle on his own blood.

With a sudden fury Maya lunged off the bed and started slapping and punching Prance while Chalmers tried to hold her off. She was sweaty, and all he could see of her face was the whites of her eyes and gritted teeth as he lifted her up and carried her away from Prance's whimpering body.

Chalmers's ears were ringing from the pistol shot in close quarters, and Maya was too much of a handful. In the living room he set her down and shook her and when that didn't calm her Chalmers slapped her across the cheek.

Maya went rigid, staring at him, snot running from her nose.

"I'm sorry about that," he said. "I'm really sorry. Please, get your clothes. You're going home."

"Home?"

"To Leonard's."

She nodded. Wiped her nose with the back of a hand.

In a frenzy she gathered up her clothes and began to dress.

Chalmers returned to the bedroom and hauled Prance to a sitting position and dropped him against the bed. He made Prance look at him. Chalmers flexed his right hand as though he may throw another punch for good measure. Prance failed to flinch.

"You a goner, Jack."

Instead Chalmers turned and drew his service pistol and prodded the remains of Prance's nose with the muzzle. Prance yelped.

"I'm willing to risk everything I hold sacred to end your life right now," Chalmers said.

Prance weakly held up a hand to suggest he was open to discussion.

"Wait a minute, Jack," he said. "There is things going on you just don't understand."

"Humor me."

"Long as she is still alive," Prance said. "Bad news to some very powerful people, got me? I was only trying to protect her."

"By abducting her to your little sex den?"

"No, no. By taking her off the grid. This county don't belong to us no more, Jack. Been sold to private interests. They're fixing to turn it into a little *Culiacan*. No rules but their rules. Maya knows all about it. Whores and politicians, Jack, they got all the secrets."

"Been wanting to tell you for a long time now. You are a shit-tier human being, you know that?"

Prance tried to get a fix on her whereabouts. He spat blood.

"Where'd she go?"

"Getting dressed," Chalmers said. "Be thankful for the long trigger pull on that Smith. She almost turned your privates into purée. Probably should've let it happen."

"I'll give her this, she's got guts. Too bad you're both goners, Jack."

"This is something for the feds."

There was alarm in Prance's rapidly swelling eyes.

"These folks that want Maya. Shit, Jack. They've dealt with the feds aplenty. DEA, too. I hope your Spanish is good. 'Cause you are fixing to hear it spoken a lot more around here."

"Stand up."

Prance was wheezing badly. Bubbles of snot and blood expanded and burst over his nostrils. He leered at Chalmers, and then asked for his pants. While Prance dressed something approaching shame entered his face.

"Turn around," Chalmers said.

It took Prance a full thirty seconds to get to his feet. He had the shakes. Chalmers cuffed his wrists.

"Let me put on a shirt at least, Jack."

Chalmers found a rumpled tee on the floor, sat him on the bed and worked the shirt up over his head.

"The charge?"

Chalmers rattled off a list of offenses, a few of which turned Prance's already defeated mood more solemn.

"Give me a break," he said.

"You can always beat the rap, but you can't beat the ride. Captain, you are going for a goddamn long ride."

Chalmers pushed him through the trailer to the front door.

"Don't do me like this, Jack," Prance said. "Our lives are in danger. Think of your family."

Chalmers stopped and looked at Maya, waiting in the yard.

"My family?"

"You give me a chance to lay it all out, you'll understand. We can pretend all this never happened. These folks will just kill everybody. It means nothing to them."

"So why tell me?" Chalmers said.

"Figure you and I can break the case. The body in the woods, the fire at Leonard's place? We could make it work, Jack—you *and* me. There'd be some good money in it for you, too. I got ten thousand cash under the mattress with your name on it. All you got to do is play ball."

Maya turned her back on them.

"Shut up, Ronnie," Chalmers finally said. "You talk way too much."

He Mirandized Prance and put him in the back of the cruiser. Looked at the palms of his hands, as if they had become contaminated from handling the captain.

"Maya?" he said.

She turned.

"I have to ride with him?"

"Just to Leonard's. You have other plans?"

She came reluctantly to the cruiser, got into the front seat, crossed her arms, closed her eyes, and bowed her head, making an inviolable cocoon of herself.

Chalmers dropped Maya off at Leonard's house, with instructions to stay there until she heard from him. She nodded but didn't speak. No sign of Leonard, either, but there were lanterns hanging from the porch and a light in the kitchen. Chalmers hoped his uncle had enough sense to be resting. He watched until Maya was in the house before driving Prance to jail.

Prance had exercised his right to remain silent, but Chalmers could feel his eyes boring holes through the partition.

Back on asphalt they passed a Baptist church and a sign lamenting the dog days of summer that read: HELL IS HOTTER THAN THIS.

Prance finally broke his silence.

"Turn me in, and, like I said, the girl's fish food," he said.

Chalmers glanced at the rearview mirror.

"You suddenly concerned about Maya's well-being?"

"She's high priority, man. They'll find her eventually."

"How about coming up with a few names, Ronnie, you know so much?"

Prance didn't elaborate. He was still, staring out at the passing countryside.

"There's jail time, and there's grave time," Prance finally said. "I'll beat this, Chalmers."

"That so?"

"State law says police officers charged with serious crime have the legal right to appear before the grand jury."

"You can give a statement, too," Chalmers said.

"Very good, Jack. But you're only half-bright."

"Sounds like you're patronizing me, Ronnie. What happened to that bribe you offered?"

Prance exhaled. Leaned his head back and closed his eyes. A few minutes passed while Chalmers drove in silence.

"I want you to do me a favor," Prance eventually said.

"Not in any position to ask for one, are you?"

"I'm going to need protection."

"Why?"

"Here's why—you're going to charge me with violation of oath of office, perjury, accepting bribes, and aiding and abetting drug distribution. Then call the GBI's dual-purpose office in Thomasville and tell them about me. How they should look at the last five years of possession with intent cases in the county. Then direct them to the tax assessor's office, tell them to study up on property ownership up and down the river near the wilderness area and tracts bordering the paper company, plus Leonard Moye's land. Then I want you to tell them about a pimp and human trafficker named Lucio. Tell them GBI boys Lucio has dirt on half the state assembly and City Hall. Tell them Lucio moved into the drug game, wants to set up extremely remote, underground clandestine production labs and is backed by heavy hitters."

Chalmers swallowed hard. He met Prance's reflection in the rearview mirror.

"You plan on supporting these claims with some evidence?" he said. "Or just your sworn word?"

"You'll find out, Jack. Meantime better go back to my place before that ten thousand disappears."

Chalmers kept his mouth shut and drove through the nearly deserted town. At the funeral home he turned right on Nine Mile Still. The road intersected a feed mill and a sulfur plant that had recently opened. After a few miles they passed farmland, lonely looking homesteads and fields of open cotton bolls ready to be harvested.

"How much does the sheriff know?" Chalmers said.

Prance laughed.

"That old-timer is as clueless as a nun with a rubber dildo. Stayed in office long as he has on account he can quote scripture so well."

"Why, then?"

His question went unanswered. The cruiser's headlights stunned a family of does in a soybean field. Chalmers knew come December the edges of those croplands would be active with bucks, the county known among hunters for its late rut. They crossed a creek, and a mile farther along came to a low concrete building surrounded by cyclone fencing. There was an array of antennae on the roof of the sheriff's department; a few cruisers parked in front, the jail at half capacity and still as the eye of a hurricane.

Chalmers parked, turned around in his seat, and studied Prance.

"Ready?" Chalmers said.

"You motherfucker. Didn't you hear anything I had to say?"

"More than I wanted to hear, Ronnie."

When Maya saw the envelope she knew Leonard was gone.

He had left it for her on the kitchen table, her name scribbled across the front, a loaded pistol for a paperweight.

She drifted through the house, calling for him. But the bed in his room was unmade, the glass of water untouched on the nightstand. A dresser drawer sagged open, its contents removed. Maya realized the wardrobe appeared to be missing a long gun along with several boxes of the stockpiled ammunition.

She wrapped herself in a blanket and lit a cigarette. It took some time to work up the nerve. Finally Maya opened the envelope, pulled out his letter, and began to read.

Afterward Maya picked up the revolver and a lantern and walked into the yard. Half a dozen cats greeted her there, many crying for their supper. She looked out at the field and its ghostly scarecrows, hearing somewhere in the distance the shrill bark of a red fox.

Frogs in the holly trees croaked their nightly love calls as she approached the barn, moonlight silvering the gabled roof. The double doors stood open. She held up the lantern. Wondering if Leonard was in there, or if not, someone else.

"Leonard?"

Maya strained to see beyond the throw of the lantern. Tire tracks ran the length of the aisle where the Hudson had been parked. She heard a scratching sound, the clank of wood meeting metal, and jerked around, nearly dropping the lantern. Her shaky right hand struggled to hold the pistol steady.

A shadow scurried from one of the stables.

Maya jumped, cocked the hammer like Leonard had shown her and tracked an opossum across the threshing floor. But the critter hadn't drawn her attention; it was the rusty steel drum the opossum had emerged from.

Arms and legs jutted from the drum at odd angles.

Maya went for a closer look. Clothing was stuffed nearly to the brim of the drum. Old blouses. Dresses. Undergarments.

And what was left of Marjean, the mannequin's discarded limbs and torso.

Maya rifled through Marjean's clothing, removing a dress. She studied it in the light, then draped it over an arm and returned to the house.

Maya didn't need to read the letter again but she did anyway. Over and over until the sun came up and her eyelids drooped from exhaustion. She retreated to Leonard's bedroom, laid the pistol on the nightstand, and fell onto the bed, clutching a pillow that smelled like Leonard's hair tonic.

In a dream she saw herself as an old woman, combing the hair of a child while cats purred around their feet and purple shadows of twilight inked their way across the floor. Then Maya found herself in a pond among the shad and bass, crappie and mayflies and bream while Leonard explained the different types of fish. His voice was as clear as her own as she swam to a flat of lily pads, the sunlight fractured here. She thought she might drown but breathing had never been easier. She saw bait in the water, heard Leonard warning her—*don't take it, child.* But the bait twitched enticingly, then pulled back to the surface and she couldn't help herself and followed the jig head with her mouth open and took the bite, not knowing any better, not knowing any better, not knowing any better.

TWELVE

THE MAYOR CANCELED HIS APPOINTMENTS.

By midmorning the ants were crawling. The Mayor wanted to cancel his appointments but knew that he could not.

There had been no news about Lambert.

And no word from Lucio.

Just a cryptic message, relayed in private after a meeting at the Consulate General. The Mayor had been formally invited to a World Expo in Mexico City.

"These boots," a man named De Leon had said to him. "You like them, no?"

"What are they? Alligator skin?"

"The *Querétaro*," De Leon had said. "Rattlesnake. So popular among my friends."

"They are?"

De Leon smiled.

"I will get you some."

"No, no, it's all right."

"No I insist. The snakeskin boots are coming. Just for you."

Lambert's disappearance raised eyebrows. The Mayor had told those in his office that he'd granted his director of security a temporary leave of absence, a confidential contracting job overseas. A four-man detail from APD was assigned to replace him.

Desperate to score, The Mayor tried an old number but no one called him back. Lambert had been the middleman, his interference, his arranger, insulator, supplier, and enabler.

His Honor's moods swung wildly, from elation to paranoia to skin-crawling agitation, and finally depression.

The Mayor initiated a conference call with his attorney and the city's chief legal adviser. His lawyer talked Justice Department and improprieties. The city attorney had a different take on his potential problems.

A pervasive malaise settled over him.

And everywhere The Mayor looked he saw an assassin.

Drifting alone through his duties, frightened by Lambert's silence, he waded black waters of introspection.

Drowning in a fever dream.

Maya was more than a dream, however. In his wakeful hours she possessed his soul.

Making matters worse, news of The Mayor's candidacy broke. A press conference with the incumbent turned awkward. They were there to announce a new transportation initiative.

"You look like shit," the governor said. The Mayor self-consciously straightened his tie, which felt heavy as a noose.

"Just a cold."

The governor had a hand on The Mayor's back, as if he was guiding a steer to slaughter. They were walking toward a stage to address the assembled press corps when the governor whispered to him, "You picked a bad day to go off your junk."

But The Mayor said nothing, turning his hand regally this way and that, smiling big, hoping he still had a good angle for the cameras.

Later that afternoon security reported a suspicious package. First floor. City Hall.

His Honor's meeting with chief counsel would have to wait. The police evacuated the building. Bomb squad was en route. There was a well-rehearsed drill to follow.

The Mayor and two senior staffers took his private elevator. A plainclothes officer accompanied them. The cop turned up the volume on his rover.

The elevator bell dinged. The doors opened to an underground parking garage.

It was a cardboard box, a radio voice reported. Wrapped in a flour sack.

Addressed to The Mayor.

From *an old friend.*

THIRTEEN

LEONARD HAD AVOIDED THE INTERSTATE, preferring the older two-lane blacktop known to locals as the Rebel Highway. It would add a few hours to his drive, but he welcomed the slower pace of the small towns compared to the snarled freeway. Weary and needing sleep, he took himself a room at a motel outside of Cordele. Leonard rested for two days, gathering his thoughts and trying to calm his racing heart.

It had been many years since he had driven the old highway. The cotton fields these days had big green machines doing the harvesting, instead of stooped pickers, figures he recalled, hunched under wide-brimmed straw hats, dragging their sacks down the long rows. It was hard labor to kill a man's back and dim his spirits. Leonard had once picked thirty pounds as a teenager, a full day's work he swore he would never repeat.

Crossing the coastal plain, Leonard marveled at the agrifarms, the shiny metal grain bins and machinery sheds. Homesteads with wraparound porches, picturesque shade trees, cow ponds and fenced-in side yards. There was more development than he remembered, clear-cut after clear-cut, logging trucks rumbling down the highway. No thought of what it did to the wildlife. He drove long stretches of countryside, lonely sights, of farmhouse ruins and shotgun houses blanketed with kudzu, or hand-painted signs for churches promoting their brand of apocalypse.

He drove through Mount Olive, a town he had not visited in thirty years. Happy to see the taxidermist was still open. So was the hardware store, a mural for Bull Durham tobacco ghosting one brick sidewall. A barbecue joint down the block was doing brisk lunch-time business, and Leonard was of a mind to pull over and eat but decided to press on.

Two hours south of the city he spotted a fruit and vegetable stand and pulled over, mopped his forehead with a handkerchief. He took a sip from a canteen he'd brought with him. A rusty old water tower loomed in the middle distance. The air was dry and hot and the sun hung in the sky like an ingot.

A woman sat under the slanted roof of a shed, fanning at gnats, raising a cigarette to take a fitful drag. She had one lazy eye and a precancerous tint to her skin. A wrinkled neck Leonard thought you could lose a nickel in.

She was listening to Roy Acuff on a tiny portable radio. There was an array of seasonal vegetables around her. Her hand-painted sign advertised boiled peanuts, butterbeans, shelled peas. She watched Leonard, squinting with the good eye as he approached.

"Hidy," she said. "My, if you don't look familiar."

Leonard tipped his hat and grimaced at the sun in his eyes.

"Reckon on how I can get to the Moye place?"

"Moye? Huh. Well, now you can't go like you used to on account the road's being constructed on."

"That's why I'm asking," he said patiently.

"All right then."

She studied him with fresh interest.

"Wouldn't be kin to Percy, would you? Or Marjean?"

"No," he said, thinking the woman's voice had a malicious tone when she pronounced his ex-wife's name. "I'm just an old friend."

"Old friend?"

She smiled.

"You knowing her husband?"

Leonard looked away. A hawk was in a leisurely holding pattern over a field to the east. Somewhere a diesel engine fired up.

"Long time ago I did."

The woman nodded, screwing up her face as she pointed to the stop sign behind her. A dirt road slanted from there into the woods.

"Take that fork, honey," she said, "Until you come to the old grain bin and then you'll make a right. It's about a mile on. Can't say there's much left. Last I heard Percy Moye done sold the business and most of the land. He's been in a real bad way."

Leonard wiped his face, and then pointed to the three massive watermelons resting on a bed of straw by the woman's feet.

"Them look like they deserve blue ribbons," he said.

She bobbed her head proudly.

"Buyin' one, I'll give you the second for half money."

"Maybe on the way back."

"I never close," she said. Then she produced a pint of whiskey and offered the bottle to Leonard to seal the bargain he'd hinted at. "One old bat to another," she said gaily.

Leonard shook his head, tipped his hat again, and drove away.

He found what remained of his brother's farm with no difficulty.

There was a dogtrot barn that sat back from the road, the breeze-way blocked by vines and unchecked weeds, a rusty tiller nearby but no tractor in sight. Weathered sign for a HVAC outfit, the prefab metal shop gone to ruin. A pumphouse and tarpaper home were the only other buildings.

Looking at the modest spread, Leonard had several thoughts, and very few of them were good. He couldn't help feeling satisfaction at seeing such a miserable existence for Marjean while he'd gone on living in relative comfort, never without, never burdened with the fierce poverty of everyday life.

They deserve this, Leonard told himself.

There was a battered pickup parked in the front yard. A man about forty was unloading a basket of produce, bread, and a gallon of milk. Two children, a boy and a girl, chased each other up the dusty drive, the black-haired boy wielding a switch, much to his sister's dismay.

Marjean watched from the porch, hands joined behind her, smiling at her grandchildren.

Leonard parked on the side of the road about thirty yards away. He considered driving on, because a terrible depression had come over him, of time lost and time wasted on two lives.

But after a few moments he got out and walked toward the house. A sandy-colored mutt barked a warning. Leonard hesitated by the mailbox, feeling Marjean's unfriendly eyes on him. The young man named Joshua turned and watched him as well. Leonard respectfully took off his hat, looking at Marjean.

"Is that who I think it is?" Joshua said.

She kissed Joshua on the cheek, the gesture belying her blank expression.

"It's all right. Gather up them kids and tell your daddy goodbye."

Leonard didn't move. Joshua called to the children and soon after they disappeared with him inside the house. Marjean and Leonard regarded each other like two fighting dogs, silent in standoff until her son came out of the house again, looking at his mother, then a longer look at Leonard.

The dog jumped up onto the flatbed as Joshua promised to come by the following day. His children were loud and showing only casual interest in Leonard. He couldn't help but see something of himself in the little boy, Marjean in the girl.

Marjean's son hesitated, glancing again at Leonard.

Then he got into his truck and drove away.

When the pickup had disappeared down the road, Leonard, hat in hand, crossed the yard and stopped at the foot of the porch.

"I was in the neighborhood."

He scanned the knee-high grass. Leaf cutter bees were swarming all over the yard, on the wing for just a few more days, he figured.

Marjean smiled bitterly.

"Liking what you see?" she said.

She had aged considerably. Her hair was thin, face pale and etched with the worry and trials of a caretaker. She rubbed a kidney as if it pained her, and Leonard could see arthritis had doubled the size of her knuckles.

"I heard as how he's bad off," Leonard said.

"Heard from who?"

"Woman at the vegetable stand."

"I suppose that old hag told you how to find us?"

"She did. But it was Jack actually."

Marjean shook her head and looked back wearily to the house, one hand braced on a porch pillar.

"You hear from him?"

Leonard nodded.

"We were recently reacquainted. He's doing fine."

"Well, his daddy's dying. I suppose you want to see him?"

Leonard shrugged, at a loss and surprised by the anger he still felt. He balled a hand into a fist and then relaxed it. Marjean's cheeks caved briefly as she worked her dentures back into place.

"What is it you want then?" she said.

"I come to tell you something."

"After half a lifetime you decide you got to tell me something I want to hear?"

Leonard felt his heart palpitate. He took a breath that sounded like a gasp, as if the air didn't want to stay in his lungs. Marjean's eyes narrowed.

"You all right yourself?"

Leonard shook his head.

"Never could let you go. Let go of this life I imagined for myself—for the two of us. A life I could never realize. I've been a cold-hearted son of a bitch most of the way," he said. "A little light in the head, I admit. But that don't mean I deserved what you done to me."

She looked back into the house again. They both heard Percy, a coughing fit turned to a plaintive outcry from a bedroom on the first floor.

"You, me, and your brother, we're on our way to being ancient history," Marjean said. "I couldn't take no more of you, so I dealt myself a new hand. Simple as that."

"Your kind of dealing don't get easier with time."

"If what you're wishing for is an apology, keep wishing. Meantime, shit in your other hand, Leonard, and see which one fills up first."

"You're still mean enough to nail up Jesus, you know that?"

Marjean's face eased some, almost relaxing in a smile. If she had been holding a shotgun, Leonard thought, it was as though she had thumbed the safety back on.

"None of us can change what happened," she said. "So be on your way, Leonard. If you got a place to go."

He nodded.

"So happens I'm nearing the end of a journey."

She looked a little surprised at hearing such a thing from him.

"A *journey?*"

"Looking back on the things I've done in my life, maybe I deserved to lose you, deserved to live alone. Hating you and Percy, hating the world, and everything in it I set eyes on."

"Hate can make us crazy," Marjean said. "You brought it upon yourself, Leonard."

Her eyes began to tear. She used a threadbare sleeve to pat them dry, and then shook her head at Leonard in apparent disappointment.

"Never was proud that I run off with Percy. He had his flaws, but I fell deeply in love with him. What you and I had wasn't love. It was fear. But you don't scare me anymore. Live long enough and nothin' does."

Leonard fingered the brim of his hat. Tried to picture his older brother in the house, bedridden, and slowly suffocating. His own heart had a peculiar offbeat gallop to it. He thought of the pills in his pocket but didn't want to take them out in front of Marjean.

"Just wanted you to know that you've been with me all these years," he said. "And that I still have love for you and Percy despite all."

"Now's that a pretty sentiment. Why don't you go ahead and die now—just don't do it in my front yard."

She turned to go back in the house.

"Wait, Marjean. Marjean—?"

"What is it?"

"A young person has come into my life," he said. "And I have tried to help her. Tried to do the right thing even if it meant killing men."

Marjean froze and looked at him. Offered Leonard an angry snap of her hand.

"I don't want to hear this."

"Yes, you do. And you will. Now I don't believe in the afterlife. Only the mark we all leave on this earth. I'm here to tell you I'm about to leave my mark. And that I hope what days you have left they are lived in peace, Marjean."

He hesitated as if there was something else to be said. Her eyes were wet again.

Leonard put on his hat and tipped the brim, then turned and walked across the yard, bees darting around him.

Marjean called out to him once. Too late, as he drove away.

Leonard stopped at the fruit and vegetable stand as he had promised and bought boiled peanuts, one of her watermelons, and some large green scuppernongs. The muscadines were ripe, juicy, and if anyone had intentions to track him, Leonard figured they could follow the trail of seeds and shells he spit out the window as he drove north toward the city.

He stopped to fill the Hudson's tank at a service station outside Luthersville. He felt better with a full belly. That and the lightened conscience his visit to Marjean had provided.

He thought about Maya, reckoning she ought to be safe if Chalmers had anything to say about it. Hoping she would forgive him for leaving without a personal goodbye.

After wrestling with honesty his whole life, Leonard felt ready and able to tell the truth.

Closer to the big city, the towns tended to merge, an uncanny sameness about them all. The clutter—so many people, and more being born every day—amazed Leonard. Car dealerships were everywhere, and fast-food restaurants and strip malls. The Rebel Highway, once the state's only north-south artery, had now been deemed historic, quaint, just four lanes of traffic interrupted by countless stoplights. He could recall the desolation of that same stretch of road forty years prior, nothing but pinewoods, hill country now saturated with urban sprawl.

Eventually he came to the outskirts of the capital. Downtown loomed ahead. Approaching from the Southside's industrial corridor, Leonard saw high-rise buildings appear like fortresses on a feudal landscape.

He felt a twinge of loathing for modern times. He could feel eyes on him at every intersection, as if some alien wanderer had suddenly appeared.

Falling back on decades-old memories, Leonard circled the gold dome of the capital. Nerves wracked as he negotiated the downtown streets, weary of the sirens and state troopers. By the baseball stadium a group of young men eyed him in such a way he thought for sure he would have to draw his pistol, which he'd kept close since leaving Cordele. Horns blared, as he looked around slowly, unsure of his direction. He pulled into an auto repair garage, tucked the revolver under the seat, and asked for help.

Leonard finally found City Hall. He drove down a side street between the courthouse and government buildings. Found a parking spot across from the annex. A gated garage was adjoined to the twelve-story complex. From a park across the street Leonard watched the garage entrance for a few minutes. An attendant examined the permit of a vehicle with government plates before lifting the gate.

Leonard got out of the Hudson, read the parking sign, and then fed the meter a few quarters.

Two hours on the meter. More time than he would need.

Leonard went for a walk around the block, thinking City Hall an impressive building, boasting Gothic architecture, the façade composed of flamboyant arches, turrets on the roof decorated with crests. Cities changed since medieval times, Leonard thought, but the men who ran them never did.

Reporters and cameramen waited by the steps leading to the complex. Leonard watched them for a while. Uniformed police kept an eye on the growing crowd of the idly curious, drawn by the cameras, by the promise of something to relieve their boredom.

He walked down the street toward the annex. A homeless woman was beside the Hudson, cupping her hands so that she could better see into the passenger seat.

"Hidy," he said cordially.

The woman jumped back and muttered something, more annoyed than frightened by him. Next to a concrete bench were all her belongings, packed into a rusty shopping cart. She sized Leonard up as one of her kind and glanced protectively at her cart.

"When's the last time you ate something?" he said.

"Buddy, I don't recall."

"You like peanuts? I got some in my car if you're hungry."

She watched as he unlocked the Hudson and retrieved the sack of boiled peanuts from the dash.

Leonard offered her the sack. She hesitated, suspicious, but took it. She peeled back a wet shell and ate.

"So this your car here? Seen one just like it in a movie."

"It is," he said, watching her. One side of her face sagged, as though stricken with Bell's palsy. He exhaled slowly and ran a hand across his forehead. Thinking every human being had a purpose, the plan and the maker none of his concern.

"You around here a lot?"

"I am. Twenty-four hours a day, yes, sir."

"You know where The Mayor lives?" he said.

"Sure as hell do. I was at a party there just the other night."

Leonard pointed to the annex.

"He lives in there?"

The woman laughed.

"No, sir. He lives in a mansion by the lake. That's just his office up in there."

"He there now?"

"You got any money?"

Leonard pulled a ten-dollar bill from his wallet. The woman's eyes flared like gas lamps. He counted off two more bills. She plucked them from his hand and buried them inside her clothes.

"I see him come and go every day. Like clockwork."

They both turned their heads at the sound of a jackhammer from the construction site behind them. Chatter rose from the steps to City Hall. A press conference was apparently underway.

"You know how he gets to and from work?"

"What's that worth to you?" she said.

"I got scuppernongs in my car. You like them?"

"Scupper-what?"

Leonard peeled off another bill and handed it to her.

"Right. He comes and goes right through there," she said, pointing to the parking deck. "Elevator takes him up there, across from the new high-rise. Most days he's here by eight in the morning, leaves around six. Rides in the back of a big black car. Always a redheaded man by his side. Mean motherfucker. I got too close to The Mayor once, and he kicked my ass. You believe that?"

"No other cars? No police?"

The woman shook her head.

"Sometimes police, too. But mostly just that redhead with the bad eyes. Matter of fact, they both got bad eyes. Life is a cancer, but none of us want to die? How's that for crazy?"

"We're all crazy as hell, one way or another," Leonard said. "There more than one way inside over there?"

"Through the atrium. When I bad need a toilet that's where I go. They've got security guards and metal detectors. You got to know just how to slide by, not get seen."

"So you've been inside?"

"Hell yes. All the time."

She laughed suddenly.

"What's so funny?"

"I used to be His Honor's wife, till I done divorced him for irreconcilable differences. They all know not to lay a hand on me I get caught. Name's Jane."

Leonard mulled the extent of her delusion and made a choice.

"Jane, if I gave you a package to deliver to that atrium, would you know how to get it there?"

"Not no bomb, is it?" Jane said in dark appraisal. "Though you don't look the type. But I got to be careful. Can't go by how I look, either. I'm law-abiding, mister."

"So am I," Leonard said. "It's a gift for The Mayor. A special gift."

"Well, now," she said, looking over at City Hall. Then she fixed him with a calculating eye. "What's it worth to you?"

Leonard took out a fifty-dollar bill from his wallet, gave her time to absorb her sudden good fortune. Then he folded the bill several times, making it easier to tear, and gave her half.

"The other half's for after you make the delivery."

She snatched her piece of the bill.

"Yeah? Where I find you at?"

"Right here," Leonard assured her.

"Well—?"

He told her to wait on the sidewalk, which they had to themselves. Then he popped the trunk of the Hudson and removed a small box wrapped in cloth and handed it to her. Jane looked at the box.

"What's in it?" she said.

"Not a bomb."

"Not—a bomb?"

"Ain't worth a dime at a pawn shop," Leonard said.

He set the box on a fender of the Hudson.

"I'll know if he don't get it. Just want you to go in there and deliver it to the atrium. Make it known you got a package for The Mayor. That's all. Be loud and clear about it."

She nodded and put his gift on top of the shopping cart and began to push it up the street toward the park.

"World needs more job creators like you," Jane said. "God bless."

Around the steps to City Hall the crowd had thinned and Leonard figured the press conference was over, almost before it began. Cars were leaving the parking garage. Leonard glanced at his pocket watch. Looked up and down the street. A woman walked past him with an attaché case, heels clicking on the sidewalk. A man with a brass saxophone appeared to be searching for a place to set up for the evening. His attention turned to the high-rise for a moment, at a man in a hard hat standing way up on some scaffolding, looking through binoculars at what Leonard wasn't sure.

About fifty yards away Jane hesitated at the crosswalk, and then abruptly turned right into the park and away from City Hall. Leonard leaned against the ledge, no longer seeing her in the park, figuring he had been duped. *Time for Plan B*, he thought. But a few minutes later Jane emerged from some shrubbery where, he thought, she must have hidden her cart and worldly goods. She was carrying his gift box.

The saxophonist began to play a mournful tune.

Twenty minutes later came the exodus.

And the sirens.

Jane was thinking about the money the man in the farmer go-to-meetin' clothes had given her when she came to the inter- section. Then she made a fast right turn into the park, pushed her cart down a grassy embankment to a stand of poplars favored by local addicts for the privacy they afforded. None were around today. There was garbage on the ground, an empty bottle of Thunderbird, cigarette butts, some well-gnawed chicken wings. She unrolled the paper sack Leonard had given her, uncapped a dollar can of gold spray paint, took a quick look over her shoulder, then filled the sack with paint and breathed deep.

Until her brain slowed to a lullaby beat.

Later Jane didn't remember hiding her cart and drifting back up the embankment with The Mayor's gift tucked under one arm.

She didn't remember lingering to admire the blinking crosswalk signal, filled with a kind of ecstasy from the spray-paint job to which she'd treated herself.

She didn't remember the tune she hummed, the curious or disdainful look from passersby as eventually she crossed the street, hugging the precious gift for His Honor.

She didn't remember what the farmer had told her, either, when she had asked if the box held a bomb. *Oh hell. Not a bomb? Bomb?* She didn't hear it ticking, though she dithered again on the steps of City Hall, swaying, a smile on her face.

She didn't remember a security guard coming to meet her, exasperated. Saying something to her, but Jane didn't hear. She was fully preoccupied, thinking about the contents of the little box.

Not a bomb? Bomb?

Jane held up the box and grinned disarmingly.

"It's only me," she said.

Jane headed toward the metal detectors at the entrance. The atrium was filled with afternoon light. She felt as if she were walking on air. She felt great.

Until the nagging doubt in her mind assumed force and caused her to stumble.

It was a bomb—that's what the man had said, wasn't it? And he'll know if The Mayor doesn't get it.

"A little bomb. For The Mayor."

"What?"

"Come on, Jane."

"What the hell did she say?"

Then Jane started screaming, looking at the gift box, and looking for a place to put it down.

"Bomb, bomb, bomb!"

And everyone in the atrium went nuts.

When the commotion started, Leonard popped the trunk of the Hudson again and took out a Browning over-and-under. Leonard pocketed a handful of buckshot, shut the trunk, then walked briskly across the street to the parking garage as City Hall began emptying, a horde of terrified people.

The attendant in the booth was an elderly man. He was talking on a telephone when Leonard approached. Leonard smiled at him as if he had every right to be slipping past the gate arm, the attendant gesturing and saying something but Leonard continued inside.

Alarms had gone off. Leonard passed the freight elevator and a long row of empty permit parking spots. A limousine idled in a loading zone, no driver in view. Leonard dropped to a knee behind the limo. The Browning was in two pieces. He mated the action and butt to the forend and barrel, chambered two shells, and closed the breech. He adjusted his eyeglasses and looked around.

He heard footsteps on concrete and saw a man running toward daylight at the exit. He wore a chauffeur's black suit and cap. The sidewalk was a blur of activity, people spilling into the streets. The security guard was gone, his booth empty, the garage filled with alarm bells. Sirens inbound.

Leonard ducked out of sight as police officers hurried by the abandoned limo.

Then he heard the elevator ding.

The doors opened.

Leonard stepped forward, leveled the shotgun, and said, "Hidy."

FOURTEEN

THE COP IN THE ELEVATOR with The Mayor made a tentative move toward his duty weapon. Everyone else was frozen with fright.

Leonard said to the cop, "Better think about the wife and kids."

"Okay, okay."

"Get a grip on your pistol, thumb and two fingers. On the floor, then kick your piece to me."

The cop pulled his gun slowly, stooped while keeping his eyes on Leonard and slid it across the concrete.

A woman in the elevator with the two men said to Leonard, "I'm six months pregnant."

Leonard nodded.

"I can see that. Ain't gonna hurt you, ma'am. You and Johnny Law get off now. Hustle."

"What about me?" The Mayor said calmly.

Leonard picked up the cop's pistol and motioned with it. The cop glanced at The Mayor, then took the woman's elbow and helped her off the elevator.

Leonard stepped quickly past them and got into the elevator with The Mayor. Tucked the semiauto inside his belt. Put the shotgun muzzle into His Honor's side and said, "Close them doors now."

The Mayor pressed a button and watched the worried faces in the garage disappear. He cut his eyes sideways, mindful of the scattergun. He took a deep breath.

"What do you want with me?"

"We'll talk about that."

"I think," The Mayor said. "You must be Leonard."

"And you'd be right. This elevator stop anywhere but your floor?"

"No."

"Who's left up there?"

"Nobody."

The Mayor pressed a button. Twelfth floor. Leonard coughed harshly.

"This is about Maya, isn't it?" he said, as the elevator rose. "Did you fuck her?"

"Don't be making this any worse for yourself."

A bell dinged and the doors of the elevator opened to a small alcove. A fire alarm was ringing. Leonard prodded his hostage with the shotgun, pushing him into the hall. No one else seemed to be around.

"What happened to her? Is she dead?" The Mayor said in the same tone of voice. But he had begun to sweat.

Leonard answered by hitting him in the ear with a fist. The Mayor rebounded from a wall, almost falling, as panic flashed in his eyes. Leonard felt unsteady himself, a surge of blood to his head blurring his vision for a few moments. His heartbeat became arrhythmic.

They came to The Mayor's offices. Leonard did a quick sweep, and then pushed him through the open door to the inner office, toward a desk in the center of the room. There were three opulent leather chairs and a sofa. Venetian blinds were open over the set of corner windows.

Leonard sat The Mayor down in one of the chairs. Stood five feet away, the Browning waist-high and leveled at The Mayor's head. He sat quietly, eyes on Leonard, hands joined in his lap.

"So if Maya's alive," The Mayor said, "I suppose she had a lot to tell you about me. Is it money you're after?"

"I don't give a damn about money," Leonard said. "Especially money as dirty as yours."

"I'm not afraid of jail, because people like me don't go to jail. Not afraid of scandal or shame, either, for I have none."

He allowed himself a small, ironic smile.

"What about them drug lords you're in business with?" Leonard said. "Are you afraid of them?"

The Mayor raised an eyebrow but didn't answer.

"You don't look good," he said. "You should sit down yourself."

Leonard shook his head.

"They'll be coming, you know," The Mayor said. "Three minutes, four. They'll know where to find us. And they'll kill you."

Leonard dragged in another breath, wavering. His Honor smiled kindly.

"How about I fix us both a drink? I can call off the dogs, you know? We can talk like reasonable men. I feel that in a strange way that I know you as well as I know myself. We have something in common, don't we?"

"Maya," Leonard said.

"Do you love her, too?"

They heard the sound of the distant elevator. Voices, radio chatter, someone shouting orders.

"Police are coming," The Mayor said at last. "And I am going to let them shoot you, for all the trouble you've made for me. Or, maybe I can get you out of this. Just give Maya back to me. You may think I'm a bad man, but I've done plenty of good for this city."

Leonard stiffened at a sudden deep pain in his chest. The fingers of his left hand were growing numb. He leveled his eyes at The Mayor.

"The first thing I ever took aim at was a no-account blue jay," Leonard said. "Never forget how sorry that bird looked after I killed it, how it felt in my hands. When I showed it to my granddaddy, he said: *Take a hard look at that bird, boy, because it's never comin' back. All because of you.*"

There were men in the twelfth-floor hall now, gun bearers. Leonard moved toward The Mayor's chair and prodded him to his feet with the muzzle of the Browning and walked him toward the windows on the other side of the room.

"And my granddaddy said: *'When you put your finger on the trigger, you better understand what the consequences will be.'*"

"I like it," The Mayor said. "Your anecdote, it'll play very well when I go after the gun lobby vote as governor."

Leonard raised the shotgun.

"My vote's the last one you're ever going to get."

"No, please," The Mayor was suddenly loud and shrill for the benefit of his would-be rescuers. "Leonard—I can get you out of this. Just give Maya back to me."

Leonard was standing a step away, off to one side of The Mayor.

His Honor turned his head to plead and saw the laser spot on Leonard's chest. He jerked his head toward the windows, to the high-rise under construction across the alley from City Hall.

"They're going to—"

Leonard looked down and saw the red laser dot, too.

For a second. Then it was gone.

And reappeared almost dead center of The Mayor's forehead.

The blinds over one window kicked as glass shattered and The Mayor's head popped in a bloody spray. He dropped where he had been standing, mouth ajar, eyes squeezed shut by hydrostatic pressure in his devastated skull.

There wasn't a second shot.

The SWAT team in the hall had reached The Mayor's outer office.

Leonard said by way of epitaph, "Seems you weren't as important to those drug-dealing bastards as you thought."

He sighed, and it seemed to release his essence, the ghost of him in that shadowy realm.

When the first SWAT team members entered The Mayor's private office ready to mow him down, they found Leonard Moye sitting peacefully in one of the leather chairs, shotgun across his knees, eyes still open but unseeing, his heart no longer beating. He looked in death as enigmatic as he had appeared to so many in his haunted lifetime.

Dear Maya,

I ought not to have lied to you but in my life it has not always been easy to tell the truth or accept it for that matter. You reminded me of all those reasons I despised the world but I figure what is more important is the fact I spent these years hating myself just as much. We have both seen or done some awful things in our lives, but as I write to you I wonder if our meeting meant some kind of atonement, like in the Bible?

Along with this letter you will find my last will and testament. My nephew Deputy Jack Chalmers is a good person and will help you if you are in need. Out in the field where the graves are if you dig them up you will not find any remains but what you will find is my gift. I suppose all any of us can hope for is sanctuary? I expect in death to still provide for you.

Please remember to feed the cats.

Love,
Leonard

FIFTEEN

AFTER A SIX-HOUR INTERROGATION BY special agents from the GBI, Ronnie Prance hanged himself. His weight, one bedsheet, and a little leverage were all it took.

A man who had been in his holding cell, the man with a black hand tattooed over his left pectoral, sent word from Trickum County. His job had been done for him.

Following the investigation, federal agents skewered the district attorney and the sheriff resigned in shame. Malfeasance was cited. As were endemic corruption and multiple conspiracy counts.

Not to mention homicide.

The bald man in the woods was identified. The red Bronco inventoried and impounded. Curious storage sheds near the bottoms prompted a few ponds to be dragged. Along the river corridor, hidden among flooded timber, the construction of several labs came to a sudden halt, as did the operation of a guerrilla structure cloaked in camouflage netting. Agents discovered a fleet of ATVs, waterfowl boats, a thousand pounds of semi-refined cocaine and several uncooperative men who didn't speak English or refused to.

An enterprising gofer in Lucio's organization heeded a tip-off and opened the kennel doors to a Southside mansion turned dormitory an hour before a dawn raid. Girls appeared on street corners, looking sun-starved and drugged out.

Most of them refused to talk.

An up-and-comer knew of a safe belonging to Lucio, rumored to contain photographs and video.

Basics of a blackmail business worth serious cash.

The story made headlines.

Police found Leonard's Hudson. The license plate was a phony, as were the several drivers' licenses in the glove compartment. Most assumed the old man to be an anonymous lunatic with an ax to grind. Came off the grid with a fantasy grudge.

Charges were dropped against the homeless woman. The bomb squad found a desiccated blue jay inside the box she had carried into the atrium at City Hall.

Leonard's picture made the front page of the *The Searchlight*, Trickum's weekly paper. Agents searched his home, Maya cooperative but careful not to volunteer too much information. Elsewhere in the news, a hunter spooked a pack of coyotes outside a cave entrance. They had been feeding on the remains of what appeared to be a badly burned man.

Agents left Trickum County with more questions than answers. Most locals refused to talk about somebody they knew next to nothing about.

The man with the mannequin?

Every town got one of those.

Elsewhere Percy Moye took his last breath, his share of regrets going with him to the grave. Leaving a widow to ponder the brothers who had defined her life.

There was thick fog in the morning. Maya slept a few hours, waking frequently. She would check the windows and doors, hearing phantom keys jingling, the rumble of a motor, Leonard's voice strong and clear announcing his return, assuring her she would be safe the rest of her days.

Maya drew water from the faucet and drank deeply. Then she put on her scuffed sneakers, wrapped herself in a blanket, and went outside. There was a shed with a trellis built around it, grapes ripe and ready for picking.

In the shed she found a shovel.

Maya made her way into the field. A deer was browsing on honeysuckle, the plant flowering again in early fall. The doe raised her head in alarm and then bounded away. Maya watched the animal, awed by her stealth, her quickness, thinking that the deer was the most beautiful creature she had ever seen.

She remembered what Leonard had told her, about the rutting moon, when bucks would be out searching for does in heat, the bottleneck of briar thickets and water oaks a favorite site for coupling.

There was a chill that morning as she walked across the field now, the scarecrows not so scary anymore, Leonard's tract defined by death of late and maybe, Maya thought, those unearthly figures in the field were there to scare off the dead as much as the living.

She picked up the path, remembering the way, every rock and stump. As if Leonard was just a few steps ahead, leading her, pointing out flora and fauna with the sort of pride reserved for school presidents touring a trophy room.

The graves were shrouded in mist, the markers faint and lonely looking.

Marjean and Annabelle?

He had lied to me, Maya thought. Lied to me about what hurt him most.

She let the blanket fall to the ground, and then buried the spade into the soil before Marjean's headstone. She dug slowly. Afraid of what she might find.

The dirt piled up. She heard a crack and began sifting through the earth with the spade's edge, concerned she would cut herself if she used her hands.

She found a broken mason jar stuffed full with hundred-dollar bills.

The fog eventually burned off. The gnats were long gone. Gone with the dog days, Maya could imagine Leonard saying.

She kept digging. Finally stopped to go fetch the wheelbarrow, the one by the till, get a drink of water, and feed the cats.

When Maya came back to the graves she loaded the jars into the wheelbarrow. There were more than fifty total, a few thousand dollars in each, maybe more. Maya wheeled the jars back to the house.

By noon she grew tired. She stacked the bills and put them in an old shoebox.

Hungry, Maya rifled through the pantry, finding some tinned meats and crackers. She wanted to make more of that sassafras tea but settled for the well water instead.

She held her breath when Chalmers arrived in his patrol car, looking haggard, his eyes puffy and a sleepless strain on his face. He was kind and polite, however. Maya showed him Leonard's letter. The will. A request to let his body go unclaimed.

As for the money?

"It's not the most important thing in the world," she said.

But it sure makes life easier.

Chalmers assumed she would want to sell the house. Was surprised when she said she didn't. She would have to send for a birth certificate. Get a lawyer to serve as executor. He would help her, Chalmers promised. If that was what she wanted.

A few days passed before word trickled down regarding Leonard's death. Maya didn't shed a tear. Was surprised that she couldn't. Driven by a sense of rebirth, or obligation, hearing Leonard's smoky drawl reminding her that the time to cry had come and gone.

When the police came and searched the house again Maya gave them a full name and her date of birth.

Answered their questions. Knowing it would pass.

Knowing. Knowing.

She was of age and the land belonged to her.

EPILOGUE

The first good frost arrived a day before Thanksgiving as the county returned to its familiar rhythms of push and pull, give and take, sunshine and rain. The murders and subsequent arrests, the helicopters and state agents scouring the woods received almost as much attention as Trickum's undefeated high school football team.

But the townsfolk had another curiosity to talk about. This one—a beautiful young woman driving an old Chevy pickup to the market, her scratches and bruises healed, frame filled out by hearty meals and labor. She bought chicken feed in bulk, paying with old greasy bills. Had a smile wide as the river for the bag boys and cashiers.

Without fail, Jack Chalmers pulled over Maya on her every trip to town.

"When are you going to get that license?"

"But then we wouldn't get to have these nice chats."

"How's the place?"

"Hard work. Taking care of land is some hard work."

"Takes a special kind of person to tend to a piece of property. I got that tractor running good though, didn't I?"

"You did. And I spent all morning in that blind you set up. Watching. Think I saw a trophy buck. He was beautiful."

"And tasty."

She rolled her eyes at him.

"I like your signs, by the way."

"Thanks."

"When do I get to call you Sheriff?"

"When I get elected."

"You're blushing."

"How about dinner on Friday?"

"Kelly Anne cooking?"

"She better be. I couldn't boil a hot dog."

"Tell Kelly Anne I'll bring something. How's Cale?"

"A mess. Wants a rifle for Christmas. Mind if I bring him around for a shooting lesson?"

"Only if you give me one, too."

Chalmers looked up and down the street, toward the courthouse and bank, and then back toward the pharmacy. Pretty Christmas bows adorned the streetlights. Moss swayed in the breeze. Cars and trucks passed, drivers offering kindly waves to the deputy and the pretty lady, new in town, same one their wives gossiped about at the beauty parlor. Trickum a little spot on the map, Chalmers thought.

Just a raindrop. A thread of cotton, an eyelash blown from a fingertip.

Chalmers had told her back then that it hadn't been Leonard who'd killed The Mayor. And now he shared that the police finally had a suspect, but the assassin remained at large.

—It's not over yet, is it?

—I don't know.

Maya silently rubbed a shoulder, fingering the branding scar. No regret in her face.

Chalmers couldn't get a read on her and dropped the subject. Then raised a hand in parting. Watched as Maya cranked the truck and drove south on Main Street, then hung a right on Nine Mile Still Road, Maya knowing exactly where she was.

And where she was going.

AUTHOR'S NOTE

Georgia is divided into a staggering 159 counties, but Trickum is not among them. Inspired by real locations, landmarks, and geographic features in the southwest part of the state, Trickum County and its seat are my own invention. For the sake of the novel, I have also made changes to the landscape of Atlanta, particularly to the City Hall Tower and Annex, and these embellishments are all mine.

ACKNOWLEDGMENTS

Heartfelt gratitude to the following for their support: Laurent Bouzereau, Mark Falkin, Oliver Gallmeister, and the team at Éditions Gallmeister, editor extraordinaire Lilly Golden, Cal Barksdale, and all at Arcade Publishing, Tony Lyons, John Farris and Maryann Pasante, Wayne and Diane Donaldson, and Maude Wright. Most important, thanks to Heather and Liam James.

AUTHOR BIO

Peter Farris is the award-winning author of *Last Call for the Living* and *The Clay Eaters*. Published in France to critical acclaim, *The Devil Himself* won Le Prix 813 and was an official selection for the prestigious Grand Prix de Littérature Policière among other accolades. He lives in Georgia with his family.